Isabella of Spain, Boabdil, Columbus, and Little DAVID

The Adventures of Little David and the Magic Coin, Book 5

∾

Pauline de Saint-Just Gross

Historical Novel

ISBN: 1514823497
ISBN 13: 9781514823491
Library of Congress Control Number: 2015911490
CreateSpace Independent Pub. Platform, North Charleston, SC

To All Curious Children who love to learn

BY INVITATION ONLY

You are cordially invited to visit the unique world of the Alhambra with Muhammad XII-Boabdil and eat Spanish treats with Queen Isabella in Santa Fe.

༄

WHO: Muhammad XII-Boabdil and
            Queen Isabella
WHERE: Granada, Spain
WHEN: November 25, 1491
WHAT: A supercool experience with
            humanoid robots and a political
            encounter

༄

All you need to bring is a curious mind open to science and a desire to learn about different cultures.
    Hope you will join me.
    See you in Spain,
    David

Table of Contents

ENJOY THE ADVENTURE,

David

P.S. I hope my story inspires you to love science and become a scientist, or, even if you don't want to be a scientist, maybe you can invent something and make your mark in history.

Prologue

The adventure continues...

On his way to school one day, David finds an old coin. He can't help playing with it while his teacher, Mrs. Savant, talks about Christopher Columbus. He wishes he could travel with him rather than just hear about him. That's when he discovers the coin's magic.

Soon he finds himself standing next to Columbus himself. Columbus is on his way to visit Leonardo da Vinci, the famous painter and inventor who holds many maps and charts of the world. While the two men pore over one of da Vinci's detailed maps, David meets Salai, da Vinci's playful but mischievous young apprentice.

Salai and David explore the many workshop rooms, playing with some of da Vinci's greatest inventions and solving complicated puzzles.

David takes part in one of the greatest experiments and flies with bat wings when Columbus announces he is on his way to Florence to meet Lorenzo de Medici, whom he hopes will help him finance his dreams of finding a new route to Asia.

❧

Florence is partying.

During the parade, David meets a pretty little girl named Paola, who knows all of Florence because her uncle is Lorenzo de Medici. Paola's sisters are part of a parade modeling virtues to remind people of the qualities necessary to be a good person. The ruler, Lorenzo de Medici, appears on a chariot followed by a calm leopard and a playful monkey that can't resist playing tricks and scaring the leopard into the gardens where everyone is looking for him. David gets a frog as a gift from a little beggar, and the frog escapes on Lorenzo's chariot. David puts his life at risk trying to rescue it, but Michelangelo saves him. They look for the frog in the gardens and walk among the beautiful Greek and Roman statues where David discovers the amazing ability of artists to turn stones into seemingly lifelike forms. David is astonished to see his own face emerging out of a hunk of marble as Michelangelo uses him as a model for one of his sculptures.

All the while, Columbus is walking in the gardens and talking with Lorenzo de Medici about his goal of trying to find a new trade route that could bring Florence riches beyond belief. Lorenzo de Medici is not interested and suggests Henry VII in England.

David, holding his magic coin, wishes to follow Columbus to England.

᧒

They go to London, England, where Henry VII rules. Columbus hopes Henry VII will finance his search for a new trade route to Asia.

David and Henry's son, Prince Arthur, quickly become friends while playing on the royal barge as it floats down the River Thames. David learns about British history and Henry's coat of arms, but the two boys flirt with danger when they play too close to a dragon-shaped canon on the prow of the barge.

Safe on land, the boys take part in the lavish celebration the king holds for the birth of his new son, Prince Henry Tudor. David gets to ride a jeweled elephant and a camel, watch morality plays based on the lives of nine famous people from history, and attend an amazing feast where live birds fly out of pies.

While David is having fun, Columbus tries to convince King Henry to fund his trip. Henry VII can't afford to do it and insinuates that Charles VIII of France is looking for new ventures.

᧒

Wishing to go to France, David suddenly finds himself face-to-face with a massive, angry-looking boar. But just as the boar lunges, he's saved by none other than King Charles VIII of France!

When the king puts the young page Arnaud in charge of David, the two boys immediately become coconspirators to hide a baby rabbit from the hunting dogs.

Back at the castle, motherly Queen Anne of Brittany wants David to learn about medieval French court life. With Arnaud as his guide, David explores the castle, visiting the scriptorium, the buttery, and the bell tower and gleefully exploring a maze of secret passageways.

Along the way, David learns about calligraphy from a monk, discovers how wine is made, engages in knightly games including jousting and archery, and encounters the castle's many pets.

Unfortunately, Charles VIII and Anne of Brittany can't help Columbus.

Columbus goes to Spain to see Queen Isabella and King Ferdinand.

1 - Castle Water Clock (chap. 9)
2 - The Elephant Clock (chap. 14)
3 - The Arbiter for Drinking Sessions (chap. 16)
4 - The Candle Clock (chap. 13)
5 - Peacock Fountain with Automated Servants (chap. 12)

1

David Is Attacked

∽

"**O**uch," screamed David as small oval projectiles bombarded him. He quickly put his hands over his eyes. But then he felt something hard hit his stomach. So, he moved his hand to his stomach. Then something hit him on the legs. He didn't have enough hands to protect himself from the hard little objects that kept attacking him. He felt he was playing a game of Simon Says without a leader.

"Stop," he yelled, but the missiles kept coming. He moved his hands over his eyes, over his stomach, over his legs, and back to his eyes. He ran, but he was still being bombarded, so he stopped for cover by a cart. He did not know what else to do.

"Where am I?" David said out loud. "I wished to follow Columbus to Spain, but is this Spain? If it is, it is a kooky, strange place."

Protecting his face, he looked down and saw what the hard little objects were.

"No," David said out loud. "How could this be?"

He looked down again. "Yep! These are eggs," he said. "Can eggs pinch that hard? Why are people tossing eggs all over the place? Weird!"

He looked up and saw more eggs flying in all directions. The targets were anything and everything. "In a way, this looks like fun. I wish I had eggs to throw," David said, wanting to join in the action.

"I'll throw eggs too." He looked all around searching for eggs, but there were none to be found. They were all broken.

Then he saw an egg coming at him. Instinctively, he backed up to avoid getting hit right in the face, and his head hit a wall nearby.

"I am cornered," he said out loud. "I am getting pelted on all sides. Please stop. I have not done anything."

He had to escape this bizarre war, this battle of eggs waged with exciting music and dance.

David was very confused. Thousands and thousands of eggs were being thrown at people and at things. Yet, there was loud, happy music heard everywhere, and people were laughing; no one seemed to mind getting hit by eggs.

Keeping his face protected, he spread his fingers that were covering his eyes and saw a most incredible spectacle.

Beautiful dark-haired people with red flowers in their mouths or in their hair and dressed in bright-colored clothes were clicking wooden shell castanets with the backs of their hands and dancing as if celebrating a major, happy event. Others were throwing eggs as if they were confetti while running and laughing. Still others were shaking tambourines, blowing shawns, or strumming strings on a zither or a *guitara*. People were overjoyed and in very high spirits. Children were throwing flowers in the street. Quite a spectacle!

Of all of the countries he had visited since the beginning of his trip, he had never seen so much crazy activity, so many vibrant colors, so much frenetic joy. It was insane.

Then the eggs stopped falling, but the dancing and the happy music continued.

കൗ

David relaxed and turned around, no longer afraid of being hit by eggs. He saw that he was right next to a castle, but it was a miniature castle on wheels stained with egg yolks. Voices were coming from inside. Curious, he went to the portcullis of the small castle on wheels and opened it up.

To his surprise, three very well-dressed young girls with concerned faces were sitting comfortably staring at him not quite sure how to react.

"Are people still throwing eggs?" asked the frightened youngest girl.

"No," David answered.

"Catarina, don't be afraid. We are safe in here," replied a confident Joanna, holding Catarina close to her.

"But, Joanna, you said our big brother John was coming for us," cried an upset Catarina. "Why isn't he here?"

"He is coming; don't worry," Joanna said. "Maria, I wish you had not run off so fast. Mama told me to teach the Hail Mary to Catarina. And that's what I was doing when I saw you slip away outside."

∽

David just stood there looking at the three beautiful, nervous young girls who seemed so out of place hiding in this castle on wheels in the middle of the noisy, messy square.

"I wanted to see what was going outside the tent," said the contrite young girl.

"Well, you got us in trouble," Joanna replied. "Do you realize what would have happened if we had not found this castle to protect us from the all the egg throwing?"

"Gotten dirty?" Maria said shamelessly and without remorse. "What else could have happened?"

"Mama does not want us to leave the royal tent without supervision. You disobeyed her," Joanna said sternly but lovingly.

"I'm sorry, but I heard loud, fun music and happy voices," Maria said. "And I couldn't resist seeing what that was about. I wanted to see the people singing and dancing. They seemed so happy."

At that moment, David asked. "Where am I exactly? What is going on? Why are people throwing eggs and singing at the same time?"

"Don't you know where you are?" Joanna said, looking at David stunned. "Are you *okay*? Did you get hit too hard by the eggs?"

David was not sure how to answer the question. How could anyone understand where he was from? He thought for a few minutes.

Then he answered confidently, "I was with Christopher Columbus, but I lost him. I am afraid I also lost my way."

Joanna examined David carefully and asked gently, "Christopher Columbus...What's your name?"

"David," he said with a warm smile that no one had ever been able to resist. "I travel with Christopher Columbus."

Joanna smiled back. "David, you are in Granada," Joanna said. "My mother, the queen of Castile, has just won the war with Muhammad the 12th or Boabdil, as we call him. The Moor signed a treaty agreeing to give up the last Moorish stronghold in Spain. Even though Muhammad the 12th has not surrendered yet, he will. That's why people are very happy and celebrating by singing, dancing, and throwing eggs."

2

Who Is Christopher Columbus?

‿

"**D**o you know who Christopher Columbus is?" David asked.

"Yes, of course I know him. He spends a lot of time with my parents. He is an explorer. He has lots of maps. And he has these amazing objects that locate the position of the sun, moon, and stars to help him, a sailor, find his way when at sea," Joanna said. "He is the most interesting man I ever met. I love to listen to him about his dreams of finding a new sea route to a country filled with gold, silver, and spices. So, does my mother. She listens to him and dreams. I—"

"I understand what you are saying," David said with a knowing grin. "I know him well. He is mesmerizing. He is determined to discover a new world trading route, and he will."

He knew all about Columbus. His history teacher, Mrs. Savant, talked endlessly about him and how he changed the world by discovering a new world.

"How do you know he will?" Joanna asked perplexed. "Can you predict the future?"

"Of course not," David replied. "Columbus is captivating when he talks about his dreams and his desire to find new places and new people. He makes you believe he will, and you want to follow him to the end of the earth. That's why I'm with him. I want to discover new places with him. But I don't know where he is; I lost him."

"I am sure you will find him," Maria said, wanting to reassure David.

3

David Makes a Deal
with the Princesses

〰

"Tell me, do you think Columbus is with your mom?" David asked.

"I think he is," Joanna answered. "We saw him earlier."

"If you show me the way to the royal quarters," David said, "I will protect you and take you back home."

"That would be lovely," Joanna answered. "You are quite the knight."

David helped the beautiful young Spanish princesses with their gorgeous white-and-pink gowns down from the awesome miniature castle on wheels.

"How did you get in the castle?" asked David. "It must have been hard with these long, silky gowns."

"We are used to playing in these gowns," the princesses answered, laughing in unison and happily getting back on their legs after being confined in such a small space.

ↄ∕◌

Mischievous Maria saw eggs lying on the ground down by a cart. She could not resist. She wanted to have fun. She was antsy. She had been cooped up inside too long and had been unable to play.

"Look—a few eggs," she said cheerfully. She picked up a couple eggs and threw them at the castle on wheels, which had resumed its descent down the hill being pulled by two Castilians, who were cheered by the now-singing crowd. The two Castilians had quickly taken hold of the unoccupied castle on wheels and were showing it off going down a hill.

"We got off just in time," Joanna said. "*Gracias*, David, our knight, our little savior. Who knows where we would have ended up with the rolling castle on wheels?"

Maria picked up more eggs and gave one to David. David was thrilled to participate in the battle of eggs but hesitated on where to aim. He did not want to start another war. So, thinking it was safe, he aimed it at a tree in front of them and away from the crowd.

He threw the egg at the tree and hit something that let out a loud, painful sound. The big green tree branches were in the way, so David did not see what he was aiming at except the tree itself.

David bent down and looked and looked. All he saw was something gray moving, but he could not make out the exact shape.

"Oh, no! What did I hit?" he asked uneasily. "It certainly did not appreciate getting my egg."

༄

Maria decided to throw her egg in the same place. This time they heard a braying sound.

Then they all saw the something gray moving toward them.

"A burro, a burro," said excited little Catarina. "I love to ride donkeys. Please, Joanna, can we ride the donkey back home?"

Joanna did not answer. She was busy looking at David, who seemed preoccupied.

Seeing that Joanna was distracted, Maria took advantage of the moment.

"Good, let's go see the gray burro," said the playful Maria, hoping for the same thing her little sister had just asked. "Maybe we can ride the donkeys back to the royal tent."

"No, it is not time to play," said the serious, beautiful Joanna, who, even though busy, had heard what was said. "It's time to go back before mama realizes we are missing."

"But riding a donkey isn't play," Maria added. "It's a means of transportation."

David asked, "Where is the royal tent?"

Joanna pointed to a path where the braying sound had been heard and said, "Don't you see a flag? It's topping the tent. We are quite close. Look at the path next to the donkeys. We must follow that path for a bit. We won't miss the royal tent."

"I do see the flag. It looks like an easy road to follow. It shouldn't take very long," said David. "You really didn't go very far. Why didn't you go back?"

"We were trying to catch up with Maria when we got caught in the battle of the eggs. We were trapped, and little Catarina was very scared," Joanna answered. "That's when I saw the mock castle. I opened the portcullis, and we all got in, hoping not to get hurt by the flying eggs."

"You mean, hoping not to get dirty," Maria said, correcting her big sister.

David and the three beautiful princesses started walking down the path toward the royal tent.

"Look," yelled vivacious Maria as she spotted the gray donkeys running toward them making their raspy *aw-ee, aw-ee* sounds. Amid the donkeys were white goats.

4

John's Friend Gets Bitten
by a Donkey

ꙅ

Innocent Catarina clapped her hands with joy and anticipation.

All of a sudden, there were donkeys and white goats everywhere.

Then a young boy's voice was heard saying, "Joanna."

A pause followed, and then the same voice said, "Maria."

Another pause, and then again, the boy called, "Catarina."

"It's John calling us," said Maria quietly.

"Who is John?" asked David, looking around to see where the voice was coming from.

"John is our big brother," answered lively Maria.

"John, we are here on the donkey's path," screamed an excited Maria. "I see you."

John waved back to his sisters as he was separated from them by the group of slowly walking donkeys, who were now all over the path. John was with his friends Nicolas and Gonzalo and his teacher Peter d'Anghiera. They were trying very hard to make their way to the princesses, but the donkeys were in their way. No matter how hard they pushed through the donkeys, the donkeys were stubbornly unwilling to move.

"I have been looking for you all over," John impatiently buzzed over the unmoving, braying donkeys. "I saw all of you around the mock castle on wheels, and then you disappeared. I figured you went inside the castle on wheels and that you would be okay. As soon as I could, I went to the castle on wheels, but it was gone."

"We were hoping you would come and save us from all that was happening," Joanna said. "If you saw us, why didn't you?"

"People were crazy throwing eggs everywhere," little Catarina said.

"We were finishing some serious homework right in the square," John answered. "Actually, we were studying the aftereffects of the people's reactions of the last Moor's acceptance to give Granada to us, the Christian rulers of Spain. Pretty serious stuff. It was too tough to get around all the people and the egg battle. I thought you would be safer in the castle for a few minutes. I came back for you, but you were gone."

"Yes," answered Maria quickly. "It was fun being in the castle."

"We are on our way back to the royal tent. David, who is accompanying Columbus, is bringing us back," Joanna said and smiled royally as she looked appreciatively at David.

John finally made it to where his sisters, the princesses, were. John picked up little Catarina and twirled her around in the air while Joanna was keeping an eye on antsy Maria. After saying hello to the princesses, his friends Nicolas and Gonzalo with their teacher Peter petted and talked to the gray and brown donkeys, hoping to make the donkeys move out of the way faster.

დ

Gonzalo finally picked some grass and accidently grazed one of the donkey's very long ears with his hand, while offering it grass with the other. But the startled brown donkey did not like to have his ear touched and reacted by nipping Gonzalo on the arm.

"Gonzalo, you should know better than to touch the donkey's ear," the teacher said, reprimanding the young boy. "They have very sensitive ears. They think you want to hurt them."

"How would I know?" said an embarrassed but proud Gonzalo. "My parents have horses not donkeys. And it was an accident."

"Are you okay?" asked the suddenly interested Maria.

The concerned teacher looked at Gonzalo's arm and declared him unhurt.

"Let's all go back and have a snack," Peter suggested and led the way in between the brown donkeys and the white goats. David was last in line. He was hoping to be reunited with Columbus at last. The princesses were talking excitedly to their brother, and they forgot all about David.

David did not have the prince or princesses' luck to merrily go on his way. A goat had adopted him and was chewing on his pants' pocket. He did not want to yank the pants away from the goat as they could rip. David wanted to distract the goat, so he stretched his hand in a shrub and picked up a juicy branch for the goat.

David very carefully and slowly pulled the tenacious, inquisitive white goat away from his pants by offering it the juicy branch from the shrub. The curious goat immediately stopped chewing the pants and went for the appetizing green branch.

David had been so attentive to the goat that he lost sight of the group. The prince, princesses, and their friends had disappeared from sight. No doubt they were already at the royal tent.

5

David Loses the Princesses but Gains a White Donkey

೧

It was at this moment that David saw among the brown and gray donkeys and the white goats a most beautiful animal: a white baby donkey.

David approached it very slowly so as not to scare it. "Wow!" he exclaimed. "I have never seen a white donkey."

David knew now not to touch a donkey's sensitive ears. He approached with oats he forgot he had in his pockets from who-knows-what country. He could not remember. *Was it Italy? Was it England? Was it France?* He had been in so many places in such a short amount of time. He just could not remember where he got the oats.

He gently offered some oats to the little white donkey. But the sad little donkey turned its head sideways refusing any food. It looked so miserable and helpless.

"You look so lost," David said. "Just like me, little donkey. You know, it's the first time I've seen a white donkey—and a baby at that."

David examined the donkey closer and noticed how beautiful it was: a little white furry face with pointed, white, and long, furry ears and a pink nose and mouth. He thought he saw tears in the donkey's beautiful blue eyes.

The baby donkey with the blue eyes did not say anything but just stood there looking dazed as if waiting for something.

"You are just a baby. Where is your mama?" David asked softly.

David looked around and saw only uninterested gray donkeys and goats. There didn't seem to be a mother donkey looking for its foal.

David turned his eyes to the little donkey and started petting it, wanting to reassure it that it was safe with him. He'd give him attention as long as he could.

What else could he do? He didn't know what to do with a donkey.

He found himself alone with the little white donkey, the brown and gray donkeys, and the goats.

6

Fuera de Aqui

೧

David wanted to sit for a minute, but the donkeys and the goats started walking into a grove of almond, olive, and purple-and-blue flowered jacaranda trees. Little blue eyes started following the herd of loud donkeys and goats. David did too.

Out of nowhere a loud shout was heard: *"Fuera de aqui!"*

David did not understand what the nervous voices were yelling loudly. He heard screams, and they were screams of fear.

More people started shouting, "Toros...toros."

"Bulls!" David said nervously. "But where are they?"

The happy tones had been replaced by screams of panic and pain.

David turned around and saw people hurrying out of the way and running every which way. Then he heard a thunderous noise in the distance.

The noise was quickly coming closer and closer.

He looked up and around but couldn't see anything. He went up the road a little to see what the commotion was all about. He didn't want to leave the sad little lost donkey too long. He came back toward the herd and the blue-eyed donkey, but it had disappeared.

David was surprised. "Where did blue eyes go?" he said out loud. "I was only gone a minute."

He walked and walked and called, "Here, little blue eyes; come to me."

But little blue eyes was nowhere in sight.

"Poor little blue-eyed donkey, I wanted to help you find your way back to your mama."

༄

All of a sudden, David felt a hard grip on his neck. Someone was yanking him off the path and holding him under his arm while running away from the path as fast as he could.

Then David saw dust flying and these determined, huge, black animals with pointed horns as long a person's arm and small brown terrified eyes coming in his direction.

The big man holding David suddenly panicked and dropped David.

"Ouch!" yelled David, lying on the ground in pain.

David saw the enormous, frenzied bulls coming fast toward him. The bulls seemed as confused and lost as the little white donkey. They were running fast as if pushed from behind.

David quickly got on his feet and ran. As far as he could tell, he could not go down the sides, as the incline was too sharp. He had nowhere to go but up. So he ran up and ran and ran, not looking back and hoping for a miracle. He could hear the speeding, stampeding bulls coming closer and closer.

7

David Meets Sultan Muhammad XII (Known as Boabdil)

Then, a miracle did happen.

No, it was not the bulls disappearing.

The bulls were still coming at him.

Coming from the ravine, David saw a white vision: a young, small dark-skinned man with a white turban on his head all dressed in white sitting on a majestic white horse. He was riding toward him close to the big, black, out-of-control bulls with the scary pointed horns.

"Am I dreaming?" David asked himself, scrubbing his closed eyes with both hands. "Is this Ali Baba?"

He opened his eyes. It was not a dream. It was a vision all right. A real vision. It was Ali-Baba coming to the rescue.

"Wow!" David said, excited to have Ali Baba coming to his rescue.

The man with the white turban decorated with a huge diamond in the center of it came to David, stopped his glorious white horse, and offered his strong hand. David quickly grabbed it. The man all dressed in white pulled David up on his magnificent white horse, turned the horse around without delay, and hastily got away from the rapidly approaching, edgy black bulls.

Sitting on the imposing, fast-paced white horse, David held on tight to Ali Baba, turned his head back, and saw the bulls lagging back as the horse gained more distance. He let go a loud sigh of relief while hanging tight to Ali Baba.

"Are you all right?" the man with the white turban on his head gently inquired.

"Yes. That was a close one. Thank you, sir," said a grateful David. "What is your name?"

"My name is Muhammad the 12th, sultan of Granada," the sad man with the white head-covering said proudly while choking. "I am still the king of Granada even though yesterday I agreed to one day surrender Granada to the king and queen of Spain," he explained.

"I have heard of you," said David, remembering again Mrs. Savant's history lesson on the fall of the Moors.

The sultan did not ask David what he had heard. He didn't want to know. David was happy he did not have to explain.

"What are you doing on the road up to my palace, the Alhambra?" asked the dignified sultan.

"I came here with Christopher Columbus, who wants to meet with Queen Isabella," David said.

"I see. This is a bad day to get lost," the gloomy sultan said. "There are all kinds of crazy things going on."

"I know. I first found myself by a bazaar in the middle of a battle of eggs. Then as I was bringing back the three princesses to the royal tent, a herd of donkeys and white goats got in my way, and I lost the princesses. Now there are bulls coming at me."

"The princesses? You sound lost like my precious little white donkey," the tearful sultan said. "It is lost, and my son has been inconsolable. I was looking for it when I saw the bulls coming at you."

"On this eventful day, I did see a disoriented yet calm little white donkey," David said animatedly. "Could it be the donkey you are looking for?"

"Where?" asked the suddenly excited king of Granada.

"On the road—just down a few feet from where you found me. It was following a herd of donkeys and goats," David said.

"I'll either send someone to look for him or I'll come later to get it," the sultan said.

"Can you take me to the queen of Spain's castle?" David asked.

"I will, but I am afraid right now that the bulls are in the way," the sultan answered. "By the way, the queen of Spain doesn't live in a castle, but in temporary quarters in Santa Fe, which is near here."

"Oh!" said the surprised David. *I don't remember Mrs. Savant talking about Queen Isabella living in Santa Fe. I need to pay better attention,* thought David. *Don't all queens live in castles?*

"Come and rest in my palace for a little bit," the sultan said. "We will leave for the queen of Spain's place as soon as it is safe."

৵

The sultan realized that David had had a harrowing experience with the bulls. So he wasn't sure he wanted to ask David for his help finding the little white donkey that might be too close to the bulls. He knew he'd easily be able to find it on his own later on. It was also his herd of donkeys that had gotten away, and usually the donkeys didn't stray too far from the Alhambra. Pepe was in charge. Pepe was forgetful these days. He had probably heard what was going on at the bazaar and had gone to investigate at the last minute, forgetting to close the gate. The donkeys had escaped.

"See the palace up there," the suddenly elated king of Granada said pointing to the enchanting red Alhambra set among green trees with snow-capped mountains in the back.

"Yes," replied David mesmerized. "This palace looks magical."

"It is. It is called the Alhambra," the dreamy sultan said. "The Moors built it hundreds of years ago." He paused entranced by its beauty and added, "It is a jewel. It is 'paradise on earth'."

"Are we going there?" David asked.

"Yes," the sultan said.

David could hear birds singing and water cascading in the background.

"How can one leave paradise?" whispered the young king of Granada sadly.

David looked at the young, unhappy man not sure what to say.

"How can I leave paradise?" repeated the dispirited Muhammad the XII.

"But why do you call it paradise on earth?" continued David.

"There are seven colorful palaces and awe-inspiring, scented gardens grouped together to make the Alhambra. The square blue, red, and yellow palace buildings open onto a central court surrounded by columned arcades with horseshoe arches decorated with poems. The ceilings have stalactites as decorations. You will see..." said the grief-stricken yet proud sultan. "The Alhambra is unique; you have never seen such magical buildings before. There are fountains with splashing water everywhere. There are murmuring pools of water reflecting the buildings. It is heaven on earth. And the gardens are filled with aromatic roses, sweet-smelling oranges, myrtles trees, and the beautiful jacarandas with blue-and-purple flowers. I never want to leave," said the sad, pensive sultan Muhammad the XII.

After a few minutes of silence, the sultan continued. "I did not want the Alhambra ravaged by war. I had no choice but to surrender peacefully and give it to the Catholic queen and king. In my eyes, it is the right decision. I would rather save this treasure than see it destroyed," said the disheartened sultan.

"The Alhambra looks amazing," David said sincerely, looking up at the reddish buildings that became more magical as they approached.

"I never want to leave this Eden," said the sad sultan. "And now people think I am a coward for not wanting to fight."

David felt bad for the sultan. "From here it does look beautiful," David said, intrigued. "I can't wait to see it up close."

"Its alluring beauty is unparalleled," said the sultan. "Its beauty changes with each passing hour, depending on how the sun or moonlight reflects on it. I am sure you have never seen anything like it. What is your name, Waled?"

"David."

"Well, David! I'm sure you are hungry and thirsty," the sultan said. "Let's find my son, Ahmed, and my beautiful wife, Maryam, who will gladly receive you."

☙

While he rode through the gate of the Alhambra, someone rushed to help the king of Granada off his magnificent white horse.

The king came down first, and then David.

The proud but humble Moorish king of Granada smiled and said, "Welcome to the jewel of Andalusia. Welcome to the Alhambra, my home."

It was, at this moment, still his palace.

More servants came and bowed to the Moorish king.

"Do you know where my wife, Maryam, and my son, Ahmed, are?" asked the Moorish king.

"Malik, they are at the Court of the Alberca by the fish pond; would you like me to take you to them?" asked a servant.

"No. I will find them," the sultan said. "But keep my horse ready, as I have to bring David back. First, I want to show him Paradise."

The Moorish king said to David, "Are you ready to enter Paradise?"

David's eyes widened, and he said, "Yes."

He couldn't wait to see what this exotic man called Paradise.

8

David Enters the Sultan's World

ح

What could be so different about this castle than the castle of Henry VII of England or the castle of Charles VIII of France? Those castles were fun, thought David, admiring from a distance the first colorful pink and yellowish buildings in sight.

The Moorish king and David walked on a narrow path, passing under big, shady trees with twisting branches full of purple, yellow-green, and white fruits that looked like pears or tear drops hidden among big bright-green leaves.

The Moorish king stopped, touched a few fruits, and—even though a king—picked a few soft, ripe ones and gave one to David.

"Here, try one of the Alhambra's best fruits," commanded the exotic-looking king.

"What is it?" asked David indecisively, looking at this unknown, purple fruit.

"It is a fig," answered the handsome, dark-skinned king with a double-pointed beard. "Do you have any idea how to eat it?"

"Like an apple?" answered David uncertainly.

"Not exactly like an apple," the sultan answered, giving David a fig. "Actually, it is pretty simple. Look and follow my example. Split the fig in half."

"Okay," David said, splitting the fig.

"See the tiny pink seeds?" the sultan asked, pointing to the seeds. "That's what you want. Now push the fig inside out, so that you only bite the inside. It will be easier to eat the fig that way."

David pushed the fig inside out. He was curious about the fig but unsure if he was going to like it, so he very carefully dipped the tip of his tongue in the juicy fig.

"It is sweet. Not bad," said David, ready to eat half of the fig. He bit into the inside of the fig and swallowed it.

"Isn't it good?"

"Hmmm! Better than I thought," he said, eating the second half. "But you are eating the whole thing, even the peel."

"Yes," replied the young Moorish king. "You can eat the whole fruit—peel and all. You just need to be careful not to eat the white sap. It will burn your tongue a little."

॰⌒७

The exotic, young Moorish king and David continued walking on the serpentine, aromatic, and arcaded paths bordered by red pomegranate and sweet-scented orange trees. There was water running everywhere in little channels along the paths or in fountains or pools. There were gardens of fragrant pink, yellow, blue, purple, red, and orange flowers everywhere you looked and only small glimpses of the towers that seemed intrusive and reminded one of the outside world. David felt like he was someplace special; he thought he was in the Garden of Eden.

There was no one in sight. Baffled, David asked, "Such a big place. Where is everyone?"

The uncomfortable Moorish king kept his eyes on the ground and replied, "Only a few have remained. Most people have left Granada for safer villages. They are afraid of the Catholic king and queen. Only my family and those closest to my family have remained to serve us."

Silently they walked under a bright-yellow sun in a noiseless place, except for the whisper of the soft wind in the green trees and the metallic murmur of silvery water sliding in the little channels. They came to one of the towers and walked through a giant horseshoe archway where the Moorish king pointed at a marble hand carved on one side of the archway wall and on the opposite side a key saying that these symbols were important to his people.

But the Moorish king did not explain the meaning any further. Why wouldn't he say more? David was dying to know about the hand and the key but decided not to ask.

David looked up and absorbed everything he saw. They exited the tower by a smaller gate with a horseshoe arch decorated with colorful tiles. David was wondering why all these arches so far were in the shape of a horseshoe. Once more, he did not want to ask. The preoccupied Moorish king was in a hurry and walking fast.

Again they walked on a path among sweet-smelling orange trees and fragrant roses, and then they heard a strange sound. David stopped, but the Moorish king didn't.

Through the foliage, David could see an enclosure with exotic animals. That's where the sound came from. David wanted to go closer.

"Come, David. There are only a few animals left in the menagerie, and these are antelope," the Moorish king said in a hurry. "Maybe you can come back later to have a look?"

To David's delight, a little brown antelope with huge brown eyes came to the corral's fence very close to where he had stopped.

He wanted to give it some grass, but the king had spoken. He left without giving it anything. He needed to follow the king.

C✦ꝋ

They continued to a place where beautiful trees surrounded a huge well.

The Moorish king stopped briefly and showed David the well. "This well has the best water in the world and serves all the needs of the Alhambra."

David said, "May I?" Then David pulled a rope holding a basket of water and drank it. "It is the best water I have had in a while. That felt good. I was thirsty."

ᴄᴐ

They left the well and went through a corridor leading to a small open door in a building. They walked through it.

Immediately David stopped and stood in awe. It was magical.

He had never seen anything like this in his life. In front of him, in the blue water of a giant pool were crocheted arches supported by thin columns and a tall tower united by real arches also supporting thin columns and a tower above. The reflection and the reality were forming one unusual picture.

"Wow!" exclaimed David. "Unreal!"

In the giant, shiny silvery pool surrounded by red-colored buildings with arches and columns, David saw big goldfish swimming contentedly and completely ignoring what was happening outside their world, finding pleasure by swirling happily under cascading water that flowed out of fountains at each end of the long pool. Trees lining the pool acted as if they were guarding the precious goldfish in the blue pond by separating them from the harsh reality of the cold stone wall.

ᥫᑎ

In the serene pond of goldfish, David suddenly saw the reflection of a dark, mean-looking figure. He lifted his eyes, but there was nothing there. The figure had disappeared. David trembled with fear.

"Did you see a man just now leaning in the water?" David asked the Moorish king, shaking.

"No," replied the Moorish king calmly. "It's just me and you."

Uneasy about seeing a strange, dark figure in the pond, David couldn't wait to leave the magical goldfish pond.

Am I safe here? he wondered.

After a few seconds, David thought, *Is this the man that saved me from the raging bulls?* If it was, then maybe he was okay in this eerily quiet place.

9

David Spills Water —Will It Stop the Amazing Castle Clock?

❧

As they were about to walk under a portico leading to a building, David stopped at a monumental structure.

"What is this cool structure?" David asked the sultan, pointing to an impressive eleven-foot-high gold-and-blue arch whose top was decorated with two rows of doors. The top row had twelve golden doors topped with a half circle showing six zodiac signs above it. On the ground in front, under the arched structure with twelve illuminated dials were five life-sized musicians.

"Isn't it beautiful?" the sultan said. "The sun, the moon, and the stars move, and the five musicians play music. It's an astronomical clock."

"It almost looks like it's part of the castle."

"It is," the sultan answered. "It is my most impressive castle clock. It was designed by Al Jazari."

"How can the musicians move?" David asked, curious. "You don't have electricity."

"Water," the sultan answered.

"How can water make everything on the clock move?" David asked.

"It's complicated and simple at the same time," the sultan said. "Al Jazari was brilliant."

"I have never heard of Al Jazari," David said. "Who is he?"

"Al Jazari was the most creative man of his time," the sultan said. "He was a clever Muslim scientist who invented over one hundred incredible gadgets; a lot of them are activated by the power of water."

"Wow!"

"Water plays a big part in the Alhambra. Its water system was designed using his techniques," the sultan said.

"I see water everywhere," David said. "I see as much water as I see buildings."

"Because of the plentiful water, it was easy for my scientists to reproduce several of his inventions here at the Alhambra. If you are interested, I will show them to you."

"Of course, I'd love to see what else he has invented," David said. "I love gadgets. I am always collecting and trying to build new things, but I never thought water could activate objects except watermills."

"You are such a bright and open-minded little boy," the impressed sultan said. "No wonder you are interested in everything you see. You will be very successful."

"Thank you," David said.

❧

"This clock is my favorite clock because it does many things besides telling time," the sultan said. "It shows the zodiac signs and the solar and lunar orbits."

"Why are there musicians?"

"They play music on the half hour and on the hour," the sultan replied. "It adds character to the clock."

"The drummer is as big as I am," David said.

David went to stand by a musician who was as tall as he was holding a drum.

"How does the clock work?" David asked, fascinated by this huge clock flanked by two falcons standing over a huge vase.

"It works with the flow of water," the sultan said.

❧

Noise was heard from behind the clock.

"What's that noise?" David asked and immediately went to investigate.

A man standing by a tall, cylindrical reservoir and several buckets of water was carefully holding and counting bronze balls.

"What are you doing with those balls?" David asked the busy man who seemed in a rush.

"I have to load up the balls on the slots above the musicians, so that when the hour strikes, the falcons will have balls to spew out into the vase below," the sullen, gray-turban-headed man answered. "And it is almost time for the hour to ring."

೧

As David tried to make sense of all that he saw while looking up at the cart, the doors, the pulleys, and the reservoir, he tripped over one of the buckets of water, sending the water all over the white marble floor.

This caught the gray-turban-headed man off guard, and he dropped a bronze ball, screaming an unintelligible word angrily and giving David a mean look while shooing him away.

Embarrassed and scared, David ran away as fast as he could from the incensed man and returned to the front of the castle clock.

"Why is this man angry with me?" David asked the sultan. "I didn't spill the water on purpose. It was an accident."

"I am sorry," the sultan said sincerely. "The hour is about to strike. The servant is very meticulous about making sure the clock works on time. He is nervous he might now be delayed, causing the clock to give the wrong time."

"I am sorry," David said, sounding troubled.

"He has to check every detail carefully, and he needs to refill water missing in the reservoir," the sultan continued. "Without the right amount of water, the clock will not work properly. He is going to have to go get more water. Don't feel bad, everything is going to be okay."

David let out a sigh of relief.

༄

"How does the water make the clock work?" David asked curiously.

"I am not sure exactly how," the sultan said. "I am not a scientist, but let me try explaining what I know. The power comes from the main reservoir of water that has a float that moves down. As the float moves down, it triggers the various mechanisms of the clock, and then the water flows out of the reservoir into a tank below the clock. Now watch—it is almost two o'clock."

"What am I supposed to look at?" David asked. "I see the doors, the falcons, and the musicians."

"Look at the crescent moon," the sultan said. "It is a pointer that goes along the top making the golden door open every hour. When the pointer reaches between two doors, watch what else happens."

ᥣ᠊ᢒ

Two o'clock.

The door opened.

"There is a man in the door," David shouted elatedly. "And the door below him opened too. And the falcons moved forward spreading their wings."

"And..." the sultan added.

"That's where the brass ball belongs!" David said, watching as the falcon's beak dropped the ball into a big vase in front of them making a clanging metallic sound. "Is the vase made out of metal?" David asked.

"No," the sultan replied. "There is a cymbal in the vase, and when the brass ball hits it, it sounds the hour."

"Wow! The drummers are beating their drums and the trumpeters are sounding their trumpets too," David said in awe. "That's a great way to tell time even though they are pretty loud. And all this is activated with water?"

"Yep," said the sultan. "The clock works differently at night because the noise is too loud and would wake people up, so the servant does not put the fallen bronze ball back until morning. So you see the servant is very busy throughout the day, also readjusting the pulleys, the men, the sun, the moon, and the spheres of the zodiac. He is a busy man, working day and night."

One of the bronze balls had rolled to the front of one of the trumpeters, so even though David was afraid to be screamed at, he picked it up and went to give it to the uptight and unsociable servant.

"I am sorry about spilling the water," David said. "I didn't mean to make your job harder."

The dour servant picked up the ball and said, "Thank you. I was looking for it."

10

David Impresses the Sultan

∼

They left the annoyed and busy servant and the castle clock.

They walked under a very tall portico into the Hall of Ambassadors in the huge Comares Tower, where the Moorish king's golden throne was. There were three windows on each wall with smaller windows higher up. The room was remarkable.

As David looked up at the sixty-foot-high domed ceiling decorated with the seven heavens of the Islamic cosmos, he almost bumped into the sultan's throne.

"Sorry, Sultan," David said, regaining his balance. "I wasn't paying attention. I should have told you I have a tendency to trip over things."

The silent king wasn't paying attention to David. He had other things on his mind. He paused in front of his throne and let go a sigh, knowing his days were numbered as the master of the Alhambra and king of Granada.

❧

David was taking in the sight of this incomparable room.

The reception hall was filled with beautiful, richly colored almost-floor-level divans covered with magnificent red silk embroidered in gold and silver, as were the hundreds of cushions resting on them waiting for people to come and lounge.

❧

"Oh! Look at the astrolabe!" said David, pointing to the brass circle sitting on a table with a silver tea set under a huge chandelier. "I know the astrolabe is used to observe the position of the stars."

David went to the brass instrument and looked at it. "I wished I knew how this astrolabe worked."

Then he spotted a celestial globe. "Again, I know this instrument. It is a celestial globe because it shows the stars, but I'm not sure how this works either. I guess it would help to know the name of the stars."

The Moorish king stopped his walk. He was impressed by David's knowledge and interest in the instruments relating to astronomy. He said, "Come with me. I want to show you something extraordinary that my friend, the chief astronomer, is building on top of the tower."

11

The Observatory and the Ancient Astronomical Computers

❧

They walked all the way up the tower and entered a huge room with a round dome. Tables with all kinds of instruments occupied every single space.

"The dome above us opens and closes," the proud sultan said. "The astronomers open the dome to study the stars."

"Too bad it is still light out," David said. "I would love to look at the night sky."

David was very excited to enter an observatory. He had never been in one.

"Here in this room, the observatory, astronomers study the moon, the stars, and the sun with the help of an observation tube, among other instruments."

"You mean a telescope," said a very confident David, proud of his knowledge.

"Never heard of a telescope," said the Moor not wanting to know more and pointing at what David called a telescope. "They just use these tubes to look at the sky and use star catalogs and many other instruments."

Disappointed by the Moorish king's lack of interest in what he had to say, David kept quiet. He so wanted to tell the king that he knew something about astronomy, even though he was young. But the Moorish king did not want to know about the telescope; he was too proud of all the instruments that his observatory held.

The king pointed at the different-sized tubes next to a star catalog containing solar, lunar, and planetary tables that his astronomers were studying and to which they were adding their own notes. By the observation tubes and charts were all kinds of weird and intriguing metal objects.

Even though David did not know the names of the instruments, he was fascinated by all of them. He wished he could get some of them to add to his collection of treasures.

❧

"This is another room filled with unusual gadgets," David said.

"Here are more astrolabes by the celestial globes, sundials, and more instruments," the sultan said, pointing to the instruments. "I have to admit that I don't know all the names of the objects you see in this room. What I do know is that they are used to observe the sky."

David was intrigued by all that he saw. But the astrolabes captivated him the most because they looked like watches with subdials. There were dozens of them in all sizes.

The Moorish king picked up a small brass astrolabe and gave it to a surprised David.

"You seem fascinated by the astrolabes," the sultan said. "Keep this one."

"Thank you, Sultan," said a beaming David. "I'll take care of it, and maybe one day soon I'll use it to look at the stars. It will remind me of the Alhambra."

"Perhaps one day you will find something in the sky like a star and name it for me," he said, laughing.

It was the first time the king had showed any joy. David laughed with him.

౼ఄ

On another table were some discs made of metal showing engraved stars. There were attached double circles sitting one on top of the other.

David picked one up and started moving the small disc to the right. As he rotated the disc, he could see different stars around the North Star and numbers on the bigger disc.

"What's that?" David asked, pointing to the two superimposed rotating discs he was holding. "Is that an astrolabe?"

"A planispheric astrolabe," answered the king. "It tracks the movement of stars and constellations across the sky. You can rotate the disc showing the stars and the bigger disc showing the dates, and you will see what stars will be part of the sky on that date. This is my simple explanation of it, though it's much more complicated."

"You are a king, yet you know a lot about astronomy. You sound more like a scientist," said David, filled with respect and admiration for the king about to lose his kingdom.

"Astronomy is part of who I am," the humble sultan said. "The reason astronomy has always been important is because my people's survival depends on our knowledge of it. You see, when living and traveling in the desert, one must rely on the stars to find one's way, or one can die. Reading the stars is a must, so astronomy is crucial," replied the knowledgeable Moorish king, who was now eager to continue his explanations of other instruments.

❧

"See the instrument there next to the planisphere? It is an equatorium invented by an Arab. It finds the positions of the moon, sun, and planets."

"They look alike. What's the difference between an astrolabe and an equatorium?" asked an inquisitive David.

"Well, they both track the position of the stars, but the equatorium easily tracks the movement of the stars and the planets without calculation," the sultan answered. "That's all I know."

David looked at the equatorium carefully but couldn't tell the difference.

∾

The Moorish king went to the window overlooking a green valley and stopped by an enormous instrument in the shape of a triangular bow glancing at the sky. Curious, David came to examine this huge device that looked like a complicated triangular bow.

"What is this thing called that's aiming at the stars?" David asked, standing by the enormous bow and examining it.

"It is a sextant," the sultan answered.

As the king was about to explain that the mural sextant measured the angle of an object in the sky and on the horizon, a most graceful and elegant but not small bird with a white head, reddish-brown body, and forked tailed flew in and onto the king's white turban. It held a frantic little gray mouse in its yellow beak and settled there as if it were home.

After a few seconds though, it became apparent that the red kite was not comfortable. And neither was the sultan, who didn't like having animals on his head.

David, who was looking outside, turned around to look at the sultan and asked, "Did I see a red bird come in through a window?"

"Yea, you sure did."

"Well! Look at that!" David said, amused to see the bird with a mouse in its beak. "I don't think the bird is comfortable on your head. It's wriggling a lot."

The big chestnut bird seemed confused, and so was the Moorish king, who hated mice. He didn't dare move, afraid to be bitten by the flying beast happily standing on his head with a mouse in its yellow beak.

Seeing the white-headed Moorish king with the red-brown bird on his head biting the long tail of the gray mouse was quite a funny picture. David started giggling but stopped right away. He did not want to upset the already defeated and forlorn king.

David approached the ill-at-ease, pitiful king and the quiet but uncomfortable chestnut bird of prey. However, the untamed red kite did not appreciate David's coming close.

The red kite got spooked, flew off the new white nest, and, in its haste, let go of the tiny, weak mouse on the sultan's head with a piercing *meoo, meoo, meoo*, as it started to fly gracefully around the very tall-ceilinged room bypassing the open dome.

You would be wrong to think he had given up on the mouse. He was eyeing the mouse still barely alive in the sultan's white turban. The red kite was determined to get back this exciting and still-moving prey.

"Sorry, King Muhammad," said a contrite David. "I didn't mean to scare off the red kite."

"Don't be sorry," said the disheveled, jumpy king of Granada. "I'm glad the bird has left my head. But I dislike dirty mice just as much." The king twisted every which way, trying to dislodge the barely alive mouse from his turban.

"Should I get the mouse?" asked David, wanting to help the king of Granada out his misery.

"Is it still on my head?" asked the uptight king.

"Yep, but it looks as if it is waking up from its torpor," answered David.

The red kite was now flying low and close to the king. The Moorish king did not like that. It made him nervous.

"I think the red kite wants the mouse," said David excitedly, looking at the bird and wondering what might come next.

The king decided to take off the white turban. And at the same time, the big bird flew down at the king's head, his wing brushing the tip of a blue, black, and orange clock with many dials. As quickly as possible, the king unwrapped his turban. But the mouse had seen the dangerous red kite flying toward it and had fled in a hurry.

"Where is that pest?" screamed the agitated king, shaking his tunic panicked at the thought of having a mouse walking somewhere on him dirtying him. The mouse startled the red kite too, who flew straight up toward the open dome. But instead of flying out, the red kite decided to circle around the room.

With the hawk flying around, David looked everywhere for the escaped mouse.

No mouse.

And then he looked back at the jittery king.

"There it is running down your sleeve," David said, wanting to scoop up the mouse but afraid to touch the king.

Who would dare touch a king? It would be a faux pas. David knew better. This was an emergency though.

David was nevertheless confused. What was he to do in a situation like that?

David decided to do nothing but observe.

The king slapped his sleeve hard but only hurt himself, as the mouse was long gone.

The red kite had seen the mouse and wanted it. It was diving down when both David and the king caught a glimpse of the reinvigorated, feisty little mouse on the floor, unaware of the bird's downward movement. They both pounced on the little gray mouse at the same time, the king stretching his cloth turban to cover the mouse and David stretching his hand to grab it. Unfortunately in their haste, they fell on top of one another and neither caught anything. But the red kite had seen everything, and in a flash faster than the Moorish sultan and David, it caught the unsuspecting little gray mouse and was now flying out the open window.

"That solves the problem," David said laughing.

Lying face down on the hard floor, David saw another gray mouse scurrying along the wall. "Oh no," he said. *This place is infested*, he thought. How could it not be with all the windows always open?

David wondered if the king had seen the other mouse and what would happen if the king saw another one.

If he did, mayhem would ensue and another battle would follow.

But the king was already standing, proudly rewrapping the turban on his head. The pest was gone. Or so he thought.

David got back on his feet smiling, wanting to get out of there as fast as possible for fear the king would have an anxiety attack if he saw the other mouse.

∾

"I think we are done in the observatory. Let's go down in search of the sultana and my son, Ahmed," the sultan said to David's relief as he calmly dusted his white tunic while wanting to get away as quickly as possible from this nightmare of a mouse.

"The observatory is filled with incredible instruments," said David, exhilarated at having seen so many new and interesting things.

The Moorish king looked preoccupied and stopped talking about all the objects. He needed to wash his hands. He looked around and didn't see any basin close by. The Granadian king didn't want to appear spineless, so he simply said, "Let's go wash our hands of all this dirt. And I know exactly where to go. You will get a kick out of this thing."

David knew the king was not talking about the dirt but that he had a horror of the mouse and felt dirty just by having been barely touched by it.

They left this room filled with every imaginable contraption invented to look at the sky.

They descended the tower, looking through beautiful arched, latticed windows at beautiful gardens and pools and ponds of water. There in the green foliage, David thought he saw an elephant with a howdah, but he could not stop to take a better look as the king was already down on the bottom floor back in the Hall of the Ambassadors.

12

The Blue Peacock

Is Serving Soap

❦

"**H**ere we are," said the Moorish king, posing in front of a big peacock standing on a bulky base backing against an intricately carved wall filled with Arabic characters.

"Beautiful peacock!" said David, thinking this big blue bird perched on a golden trunk was a little out of place against a boxed wall. Its neck curved downward with its beak pointing toward a basin as if it wanted to fetch something from it. "What is it doing here on this tiled wall against a box in this fancy hall decorated with a honeycombed ceiling surrounded by couches?"

"Wait till you see how this wonder—another one of Al Jazari's inventions—works," the sultan said. "David, you haven't seen anything like this, I'm sure. See the plug on the peacock's tail?"

"Yes."

"Pull it."

David pulled the plug on the peacock's tail and—what do you know—water came out of the peacock's beak and spilled into the basin.

"What are the two doors for?" David asked, pointing at the doors in the box on which the blue peacock was standing.

"Watch carefully," the sultan said, putting his clean hands under the beak as water whooshed out onto them. He didn't really have to wash his hands. He just wanted to prove a point. A proud smile invaded his face as he glanced at David. His peacock robot worked.

"What do you think?" asked the proud king.

The water filling the basin was now draining into a base.

"Interesting place to wash your hands," David said. "But where is the soap?"

As soon as David asked that question, a door opened under the peacock and a robotic servant came out offering a soap.

The Moorish king took the soap and washed his hands.

"Wow. Wow," beamed David, who could not believe his eyes. "Water also activates the peacock. I didn't realize water did so many interesting things."

As the water continued falling into the hands of the Moorish king and filled the basin, a second door opened and another automaton servant appeared with a towel.

The smiling Moorish king took the towel and dried his hands.

"What do you think of this other invention of Al Jazari?"

"I love it," David said, amazed. "But the servants are robots. How could it be? This is 1491."

"Maybe it's 1491, but Al Jazari came out with this idea in the twelfth century, which is two hundred years ago."

"It's incredible what this man invented using water technology," David said, perplexed.

13

A Strange Man Is Hiding
by the Candle Clock

∽

As they were about to exit the Hall of Ambassadors, they passed into a covered white-marble-floored corridor with beautiful colored tiles on the bottom part of the walls. There again, David saw the ominous, dark figure of a man seen through the shadow of the light of a candle hiding behind a pillar.

David shivered and had to ask the king who this man was.

"Sultan, who is this man standing by the pillar in front of us?" asked David, feeling ill at ease. "I think it's the same man I saw before."

"Where?" asked the sultan. He looked around but he didn't see the man. "All I see is a candle clock."

"A clock?" asked the uncomprehending David. "I see a candle. But how is that candle a clock? And by the way, I did see a man behind it who is no longer there."

The sultan didn't see the dark figure. But David had. *Who was he? Was he following him or the king? Why?*

"Yes, the candle is a clock," the sultan replied. "Don't you have lots of clocks where you live?"

"No," David said. "Maybe two."

"Clocks are important to me," the sultan said. "It reminds me when to pray."

"How can you tell time with this candle?" David asked.

"Let me briefly explain how this candle clock works," the sultan said, pointing to a candle resting in a dish that 'had a ring on its side connected through pulleys to a counterweight'. "The candle burns, and the ring on the side goes up, stopping at a number marked on the side. The number tells the hour."

"Hmmm, why would the ring stop at a number?" asked David, not seeing at all how this candle-burning clock was telling time. "I see the ring and the pulleys. I see the numbers, but I don't really understand how it works. I am sorry, I still don't get it." David wasn't as impressed with this clock even though he liked the look of it.

"I'm not sure myself what makes the ring stop at a number," the sultan said. "I just know the pulleys activate the ring that stops at the number."

"That's okay," David added, not interested in knowing more. "At least the candle lights part of the room."

The Moorish king realized David's lack of enthusiasm, but didn't know how to explain better, so he was relieved that curious David did not pursue his questioning further.

14

The Amazing Elephant Carrying a Singing Phoenix and Two Huge, Scary-Looking Snakes

ぐん

F ew people were walking around in this big enchanting, bewitching palace.

They left the Hall of Ambassadors and found themselves in the most magnificently lush and paradisial garden of yellow and blue flowers and red pomegranate trees, but in the middle of this idyllic garden stood an imposing gray elephant carrying a tower of red columns, on top of which was a gold box topped with a dome. In front of the dome was a dial; on top of the dome was a phoenix.

"I saw that elephant when we were coming down from the observatory," David said, looking with awe at this massive elephant with two long, scary-looking dragon-faced snakes.

"This is another of Al Jazari's inventions: the elephant water clock," the sultan said. "It is his most wonderful invention. There are three men, and they are very important: the mahout sitting on the head, the scribe sitting behind the mahout inside the citadel, and Saladin, the sultan sitting on a shelf above the mahout with his hands almost touching the snakes. Look at how magnificent the gold chair is on the elephant's shoulders, and on each corner of the chair is a red-marble column that supports a pale-gold citadel fortress. On top of the citadel is a gold dome, and on top of the dome is a multicolored phoenix. In front of the gold dome is a silver-and-black disc with twelve holes. That shows the time. Do you see all that?" asked Muhammad XII.

"Yes," David replied. "Do the men move?"

"Kind of," the sultan replied. "The scribe moves his pencil, the mahout hits the cymbal, and Saladin, the sultan, moves his hands toward the snake."

David came closer to examine the amazing elephant's sculpture carrying three distinctive-looking men. The mahout sitting on the elephant's neck was holding a mallet with his right hand and a stick with his left hand. The scribe, the other man, was holding a pencil and sitting on the elephant's back inside the tower behind the mahout. The bearded man, the sultan Saladin with a black turban and a red tunic, was sitting between two white falcons above the mahout on a balcony shelf attached to the tower in front of the clock dial and two dragon-faced snakes with their mouths open.

"Why are there two orange, opened-mouthed dragon-looking snakes with horns hanging inside the tower with one looking up at the man on the balcony and the other looking down at the man holding the pencil?"

"Good question," the proud sultan answered. "Al Jazari thought of everything when he built this amazing clock. Everything you see has a meaning or purpose: the men, the phoenix, the snakes, and the vases. They all work together. The snakes will drop a ball into the vase. But just watch. You will see. "

"Very cool," David said. "This Al Jazari was way ahead of his time."

The sultan smiled and said, "Good. I knew you would be able to see and appreciate."

౿౨

"There is a lot going on with this clock," the sultan said. "Do you follow all that?"

"Yea, I'm still following you," David said, waiting to hear how they all worked together. "There are lots of things to look at on this elephant. And so far, I see all that, but how does it all work together?"

"You will see in a minute," the sultan said. "There is one more thing: the two gold vases—one vase on each side of the elephant's neck. These are also important in order to understand the clock."

"Okay, I guess all these things make the clock work," David said.

"Actually no," the sultan said. "The water makes the clock work while activating the men, the falcons, the phoenix, and the snakes to tell time. So the flow of water makes everything move in this elephant clock just like it did the castle clock."

ᴄ◡ᴐ

"Now look at the long pencil the clerk is holding because in a few seconds the pencil is going to come to seven degrees on the arc and stop."

"But I don't see the pencil moving at all."

"I know. It's not time yet," the sultan said. "Just know that every time the pencil hits a certain spot on the arc, something happens with the clock. Listen and watch. It's happening now."

As the Moor said that, the phoenix on top of the dome sang.

"Oh! Look! Half of one hole in the disc on top of the clock is white," David shouted excitedly. "And then the sultan sitting on the balcony lifted his hand above the falcon's beak on his right side while lowering his left hand onto the falcon's beak on the left side."

"What else do you see?" the sultan asked.

"Now, there is a ball coming out of the falcon's beak on the right side, and it's falling into the right-side snake's mouth," David said. "Look at that—the snake's mouth tipped downward, dropping the ball into the vase on the right shoulder of the elephant."

"What else is happening?" the sultan asked David.

"And when the ball fell into the vase, the mahout hit the cymbal with a mallet, and with his other hand, hit the elephant with a stick."

"That announces the half hour and the hour," the sultan said.

"Pretty neat," David uttered.

"Let me show you the water mechanism," the sultan said, walking to the elephant's side. "Come and take a look."

The Moorish king went to the side of the elephant and opened a door to reveal the whole inside of the elephant filled with water, which acted as a reservoir.

"The whole belly of the elephant is filled with water," David blurted out. "That's pretty well disguised. You'd never know there is water in there, and the belly is huge, so it can hold a lot."

"It certainly can," the sultan said.

"Why is there a bowl held by strings floating in water?" David asked.

"Watch the bowl carefully," the sultan said.

David was watching the bowl and looking very intently at the stunning elephant clock with the phoenix, the falcons, the men, and the serpents. This was like an Ali Baba story, but the treasures were practical and captivating robotic gadgets.

"So, this is how the elephant clock works," David said. As he watched, the floating bowl slowly sank to the bottom, the bird sang, the men moved, the snake dropped the ball, and a *clink clank* was heard to mark the hour. "Has Al Jazari built many more devices like this?"

"Yes, you have seen four so far," the sultan said. "There are a few more in the Alhambra."

"I'd love to see what else he has done, even though I can't imagine what else he could have possibly come up with," he continued entranced.

"David, are you really interested in seeing more?" the sultan asked. "Because his world was fascinating, and the Alhambra has a few more of his incredible contraptions."

"I can't wait to see more," David said, feeling he was in the middle of a live science class.

"You are sure you are not bored?" the sultan asked.

"Are you serious?" David asked. "How can I be bored with all these giant toys?"

"Do you know how many inventions he has come up with?" the sultan asked.

"I have no clue," David answered, thinking of all the inventions Leonardo da Vinci had thought of. *Could he have had more ideas or invented more things than Leonardo da Vinci?*

"More than one hundred," the sultan said. "He designed automatic machines, home devices—some of which you will see in a few minutes—and musical automata using the power of water."

"Wow!" David said.

"You know, I think you will grow up to be a scientist."

"In the meantime, let's go see still another of Al Jazari's apparatus."

❧

The king had forgotten all his troubles including the little blue-eyed white donkey.

David walked through an enchanting palace with honeycombed ceilings, giant keyhole arches and doors, and walls decorated with squares, circles, triangles, and leaves. Fountains, pools, trees, and flowers were everywhere outside.

David wanted to remember everything he saw, but it was hard because his mind was traveling and thinking of everything he had seen so far. The Alhambra was more beautiful than the castles of England and France. And even the gardens of Italy. And to top it off, these clocks were like giant playthings to him.

Oh! Yes! He wanted to see more.

"Incredible," said David mesmerized by the world he was in. "All these look like giant trinkets telling time."

"You are right," the sultan said. "And what makes them move is a unique water system he designed. You know, David, Al Jazari not only created this phenomenal water clock, but he also thought of using elements from different parts of the world in his devices."

"I think I know of at least two countries," David said proudly. "India is represented by the elephant. The serpents reminds me of China. What other country is there?"

"He used the Greek's knowledge of water technology," the sultan added. "And, of course, Arab architecture. You see Arabs have ties to all these countries."

15

The Secret to the Girl
Serving Tea

❧

They were now leaving the gardens and going through more exquisitely arched, covered patios leading to a room filled with tables of all sizes and low couches in luxurious red silk ornately embroidered with gold and white, yellow, and pink pearls. The opulent walls were covered with tiles of different shades of blue and a beige-colored ceiling of honeycombed domes. It looked magical. It was a sight to behold. It truly looked like paradise.

"Everything around here looks surreal to me," David exclaimed.

❧

On a low table were fruits and nuts.

Servants came to the sultan and bowed to him asking if he needed anything. The Moorish king indicated he just wished to relax for a few minutes and show his young guest the serving girl.

"Sultan, which one do you wish to see?"

"I meant for you to bring the automated arbiter for the drinking sessions," the king of Granada said. "It is a fun one. In the meantime, I will show my little guest the tea-serving girl."

The Moorish king got up and went to the wall behind the couch. David followed.

"You see, David, in my palace there are many clocks, containers, figures, pitchers, and basins that are mechanized, and thirty of them are Al Jazari's designs," the sultan king of Granada said. "And sometimes we forget to use them. I see them being used mostly when guests come. Today, it is also my utmost pleasure to show them to you. These inventions are unparalleled in the world."

෴

The sultan stopped at a tall, beautiful dark royal-blue box designed with gold lines outlining the sides.

"It's a nice armoire," David said, not knowing what to say, but feeling kind of smart and grown-up using the word *armoire*.

"It's more than an armoire," the sultan said. "Look at this armoire and try to imagine what it can do."

The ritzy and colorful armoire was hiding a secret that the Moorish king didn't want to share just yet.

Finally, David broke the silence. "I'm thinking and thinking," David said. "You are going to think I'm not very smart after all because I can't really figure out what the armoire can do."

"You will in a minute," the patient sultan said.

At that moment, there was a water-dripping sound and something noisy moved inside the fancy armoire.

What was it? Was it a magic armoire like the magic lamp? What was behind the door making that noise?

"Open sesame," said a mischievous David, knowing that these words were part of the story of Ali Baba and the forty thieves.

The king said, "Be patient, David."

"Open sesame," repeated David one more time.

This time, the door did magically open.

"It worked. It worked," repeated an overjoyed David, jumping up and down. "*Open sesame* is a magical phrase."

A standing automaton woman servant slid down carrying a glass of tea and presented it to David, who was directly in front of her.

David took the glass and politely said, "Thank you," but of course, he was saying *thank you* to a robot, which could not reply back and had no feelings.

"What do you tell a robot when it serves you something?" David asked, not expecting an answer.

David tasted the tea. Nobody drank tea at home. So he was not familiar with the taste of tea and didn't know that tea came in different flavors.

"I have tasted that flavor before, but I can't tell what it is."

"It's my people's favorite drink," the sultan said. "It's mint tea."

"It tastes very good," said David with an honest voice. "It reminds me of mint ice cream."

സൗ

While David was drinking the mint tea, the honorable king said, "Let me tell you the secret of this armoire as you call it."

"See above the girl, there is a tank filled with tea. The tank has a hole at the bottom of it, and that hole lets the tea go into another container, and when the container is full, it drips into the glass the girl is holding in her hand. The weight of the glass sends the girl sliding down, pushing the door open and holding the glass ready to give it to whoever is standing in front of her. And that, David, is the secret to the magic armoire."

"But why hide the girl?"

"She is not hiding," the sultan said. "She is conveniently out of sight until we need her. Do you like that device?"

"I want to try to build something like that," David said. "It would be fun to have a built-in servant ready to give you a drink whenever you wanted one. My mom would love it too."

സൗ

"Are you ready to see another serving robot as you call it?" the sultan asked. "The next one is a traveling one. It goes from one room to the other and even from one palace to another."

"Really?" David asked. He was so busy looking all around him at this paradise created by men that he didn't have a chance to be bored.

16

A Rider on a Horse Is
Pointing His Lance at David

ↄ

They left the tea-serving girl and went back to sit on the sumptuous red couch with multicolored jewels. The huge and very long, delicate ivory wall cloth hung softly and undulated with the wind. Touching the multicolored, geometric shapes on the wall, it gave the huge room a magic feel.

David thought he was dreaming.

"This is another marvel. Now admire this totally automated spectacle," the sultan said, recalling to reality the lost-in-thought and very quiet David.

David was usually unable to focus for a long time unless he was moving, jumping, or exploring. He couldn't take his eyes off this apparatus now in front of him and examined very seriously the curious machine.

The servants had brought this tall, intriguing five-level fortress tower and placed it in front of the sultan.

"This is called the arbiter for drinking sessions," the sultan said.

A stunning dark-haired woman was sitting on the ground holding a gold and silver Aladdin's lamp pot with a long spout called a *dallah*. An orange goblet stood in front of her. On the stage above her were four beautiful, seated girl musicians, each holding a different instrument. On the floor above the musicians stood an attractive, dark-haired dancer. On the level above the dancer were two doors. The last level had a gold dome on which a rider dressed in black holding a lance was sitting on a brown horse.

"I thought the elephant clock was cool," David uttered, "but this is also amazing."

⁓

David kept his eyes on this new gadget, anxious to see what it would do.

"Nothing is happening," David said impatiently.

"Something will," the sultan replied.

The Moorish king grinned as he watched David, who had started to wonder if there was more to it. It was a beautiful stage to look at.

But what was there? There had to be more.

What did Al Jazari have in mind with this stage? thought David.

A servant came to whisper in the Moorish king's ear and then went to the fortress tower and looked it over, touching something on the back of the fortress.

David saw him touch something, and he stretched his neck to see but couldn't see what he was touching.

Hmmm, was there really something else? he wondered. *The fortress was impressive but...*

He started to feel a little disappointed.

But then it all started as if someone had waved a magic wand.

The unusual-looking musicians began to play their instruments, which made the striking-looking dancer dance and the strange rider on top turn.

David clapped excitedly with delight.

"Wait, there is more," said the proud king.

"There is more!" exclaimed the animated ten-year-old.

"Are you still thirsty?"

"Yes," answered David. *What an odd question,* he thought. *I just drank tea.*

"Look at the woman sitting on the floor."

David saw the exotic, silent, robotic woman fill the orange goblet with water using the gold-and-blue Aladdin's lamp pot with the long spout.

The rider on the brown horse stopped turning and pointed at David with his sharp gold glaive.

"Why did the horse stop turning, and why is the rider pointing his lance at me? Did I do something wrong?" asked David nervously.

"Not at all. Don't you see what's happening?" answered the king.

"No!" exclaimed a thrilled David once more as a mechanized steward presented him with a glass of water.

"But what is happening now?" David asked, looking at the steward. "Am I supposed to take the glass?"

"Yes," the sultan said. "The rider chose you to be served a glass of water."

"Oh! Okay," David said.

Amused, David took the glass now being given to him by a steward contrary to the previous device when it was a pretty girl handing him a glass.

"This scientist's inventions are fun."

"Al Jazari was very creative and practical," the sultan said. "Greek scientists inspired his work."

A servant brought a tray with five different little bowls of green and black olives, figs, dates, and almonds. He first offered the sultan the treats and then went to David, who eagerly took dates and olives, which he didn't eat often.

The king of Granada and little David silently enjoyed these snacks in this quiet, surreal Moorish setting.

17

Is the Yellow Parrot Going to Eat the Blue-Green Lizard?

∾

"**M**ama, please help me," a young girl screamed while crying.

The silence was broken. Mayhem ensued. Excited voices were suddenly heard. Beautiful dark-haired women were running all over, shouting excitedly, and trying to console a young girl while looking for something. They were completely oblivious to the robot serving drinks.

Princess Aixa was crying and following her mother, the beautiful and graceful Sultana Maryam.

"Someone forgot to close the aviary, and Aixa's favorite yellow parrot, Azam, escaped," announced a soft, serene voice.

"And Ahmed's emerald Iberian lizard, Kadar, is on the loose somewhere close, and you know it loves birds," added another woman.

"Ahmed's lizard is going to eat my bird," cried Aixa.

"No, it is not," responded Ahmed, being very protective of his favorite reptile with its turquoise neck and head and black spotted-green back with a long orange tail. "Kadar is way too small to eat your parrot."

"I'm sure your bird will be okay," said Aixa's mom, the beautiful dark-long-haired, green-eyed Maryam. "We will get it back quickly. Don't worry, sweetheart."

David thought her to be the most beautiful woman he had met on his trip.

"Maryam, beautiful wife, I agree with you," said the affectionate king of Granada. "Aixa, we will find Azam; you will see."

"Are you sure, Daddy?" Aixa said.

"Ahmed, please come here for a moment," the sultan commanded his young son.

The young, handsome dark-haired boy did as he was told. He approached his dad, the king, very respectfully.

"My son, we have here a guest," the sultan said. "I will take him to the Catholic king and queen in a short while. Ahmed, may I present David?"

As he was finishing the introduction, a gorgeous, frenetic small yellow bird flew all over the room and came to rest on Ahmed's shoulder.

"See, Aixa, I told you Kadar would not eat your precious bird," said the unflinching Ahmed.

"Maybe your precious bird will eat my lizard if it finds it."

The yellow bird, exhausted from all the flying, didn't move. And neither did Ahmed.

The king approached Ahmed very slowly. The yellow parrot didn't move.

Maryam approached the king. The yellow parrot stayed quietly on Ahmed's shoulder.

Aixa approached the yellow bird. The bird didn't move.

"I see an emerald lizard. It's beautiful. Is that the lizard?" David said excitedly, admiring the multicolored reptile zigzagging under the nearby couches. "What a great-looking lizard! I love lizards."

Aixa turned quickly in David's direction. "Yes, it is the lizard," she said. "That lizard could kill my bird."

"Aixa, my lizard is too small to hurt your bird," Ahmed said, frustrated. "It's the other way around. Your bird is going to eat my lizard."

"Never," Aixa said, not listening to her brother. "Kadar is going to eat Azam; I know it."

"There are lots of people around watching the lizard," David said, trying to reassure her. "I'm convinced your parrot will be fine. Look, he is very happy on Ahmed's shoulder."

Ahmed could not stay still any longer and asked, "Where is Kadar?"

Ahmed saw his emerald lizard. So did the yellow bird, and it flew toward the blue-green lizard.

The blue-green lizard had never had so much attention, so he stayed there frozen, pausing, looking at everyone staring at him.

"Everyone is paying attention to the lizard," David said, watching the parrot fly up to the ceiling. "I think the parrot is jealous and wants attention. That's why it left Ahmed's shoulder."

"Now look what happened," Aixa said. "The parrot is flying too high now. How are we going to get him?"

"Don't worry, it will get tired again and come down," Aixa's mom said reassuringly. "It always does."

Everyone stood around waiting for the bird to stop flying while at the same time keeping an eye on the lizard, which kept going in circles.

The turquoise lizard quickly got bored and started slowly walking toward the entrance to the harem.

The small yellow parrot decided to follow and do the same. Was it eyeing the lizard to eat it?

❧

The king, the sultana, the prince, the princess, David, and a whole retinue of people—of course—followed the blue-green lizard and the yellow parrot into this most extraordinary room. Its high ceiling painted gold and blue and tiled walls with arched windows gave a striking view of the green valley and distant snow-capped mountain that gave a feeling of a heavenly kingdom.

Heavenly music was heard. A beautiful young woman was playing the oud, and another one was playing a lute, which added an enchanting note to this divine Moorish paradise.

No wonder the blue-green lizard and the yellow bird felt at home in this serene room.

༄

There were other animals in the large adjoining room. Two little but elegant fawn-colored gazelles were lying on a big orange Turkish rug by a very attractive young blond woman, who lounged comfortably on a low, red silk couch.

David couldn't believe gazelles were allowed inside the palace.

Behind her was an enormous aviary going the whole length of the wall opposite a row of keyhole-shaped windows.

To the delight of Aixa, the yellow bird found its way to the aviary room, which was adjacent to the women's room.

"How many birds are in this aviary?" asked David as he spotted green parakeets with pink beaks and pink-ringed necks, blue birds with orange-brown backs, red-throated birds, and yellow birds with orange beaks.

"May be one hundred," the sultan answered. "We stopped counting after forty."

So many birds, yet not one bird shrieked. They all sang gently and chirped gaily.

♫

Everyone went to the aviary, but the little yellow parrot was not ready to go in there yet. It saw colorful fruits on the table and went for a quick nibble.

The yellow bird was fickle though. It left and went on to test the Moorish king's shoulder. Ahmed and David wanted to catch it, but the little yellow bird changed its mind and flew away.

"I hope it does not find the window," said an alarmed Aixa. "It will fly away outside."

The beautiful, relaxed Maryam said, "Why don't we just sit for a while, and maybe Azam will calm down and come to rest with us as he usually does."

Everyone sat quietly—even the young Aixa— and watched. Azam flew around and around and around but never went close to the open windows. It went to visit the aviary but left again.

Then Azam decided to visit David, who was holding crumbs from an old, forgotten cookie that had been in his pocket since Florence.

Azam perched itself on David's hand and pecked nervously at the crumbs.

David did not bat an eye. He stayed focused on the gentle yellow bird.

So did everyone.

Everyone was watching this young newcomer in awe who seemed to have special talents.

Who was this David with this incredible power to hold this bird in his hand for such a long time?

☙

Then *bang!*

A servant standing close to David thought it was the right time to capture the escapee and put it safely back in its home.

As quick as the blink of an eye, the servant had thrown a red scarf over the hand holding Azam, who had no idea of what had just happened and had not had time to escape. The little bird was captured.

The servant was the delight of the whole family but more so to Aixa, who was relieved her pet bird was safe from possible predators. She thought every animal found her yellow parrot attractive enough to eat. She watched as the servant tenderly put Azam in its proper place in the aviary and closed the door.

Then Kadar, the blue-green lizard, reappeared.

"Look, Ahmed," Aixa said happily, pointing to the lizard on the floor. "Here is your pesky lizard again."

Kadar the lizard felt totally ignored, so he unabashedly came close to the group of people in the fun aviary where everyone was admiring the birds and not paying any attention to him, the lizard.

"Now it is your turn to return to your home before something happens to you," Ahmed said, looking down at the lizard.

Ahmed bent down to pick up Kadar, but the blue-green lizard wanted to play and wriggled away.

"Lizards are so fast—look at it go," Ahmed said. "Come, David, help me. Together we will take Kadar into custody."

Ahmed and David went in hot pursuit of the show-off blue-green lizard that was having a ball going under all the rugs, couches, and tables.

18

Where Is Kadar, the Blue-Green Lizard?

∽

The servant had saved the day to the delight of all those present, but more so to Aixa's delight, who felt safe knowing Azam was back in its home away from possible enemies, who would find it attractive enough to eat.

"Look at it going under the table," Ahmed said.

"Now it's slithering under the rug," Aixa said. "It is so funny to watch the bump in the rug move."

The lizard was very quick. It had sneaked away and disappeared from sight.

"Where is Kadar now?" Ahmed asked. "Do you see him?"

"No," David answered. "He is a clever one."

They had lost the cunning blue-green lizard.

"Let's look under the armoire," David suggested.

They looked under the armoire, but he was not there.

Next to the armoire was a huge red, yellow, and black rug. Even though they did not see anything moving under it, they lifted the rug, hoping he would be there.

And there it was.

"How did we not see you?" asked Ahmed as he reached for it.

But in a panic, the scared lizard slipped through a grid cut out of the white marble floor hidden under a table by the patterned red rug.

"Where did he disappear to?" David asked, puzzled.

"Through this grid," Ahmed said, pointing to a little square opening in the floor. "I have an idea. Let's put our ears to the ground and listen."

"Why?" David asked.

"You would be surprised what sound you can make out," Ahmed said confidently as he put his ear to the ground.

"Listen to what?" David replied skeptically. "You can't hear through marble."

"Come on, David," Ahmed said. "Try it."

David looked at Ahmed, unconvinced that they could find the little lizard by doing that, but he was intrigued nevertheless and wanted to hear if one could really hear sounds, so he too put his ear to the ground.

"I hear something," Ahmed repeated. "Don't you?"

"Me too," David said, not believing he could hear through marble.

"But I know it is not a lizard," Ahmed said. "Even though it could be, but I just can't tell for sure. What do you think it is?"

"*Eerie!*" David said. "I hear *clank, clunk, clop.* Do you hear that? It sounds like someone chained up is walking very slowly."

"I hear that too," Ahmed said. "I am not sure what's making that noise though. Do you really think it's someone chained up?"

"Is there someone below? What or who is down there?" asked David curiously. "Do you have a dungeon? Does your father keep prisoners there?"

"I'm not sure what's down there. I have never been. Let's go find out," Ahmed said, looking at David. "You want to go with me, don't you?"

"Are you joking?" David said. "I would not miss going down there for anything in the world. But how do you go below?"

"I'm not sure. The Alhambra is as mysterious as it is beautiful," Ahmed said. "I do know someone who will know. Let's go find him."

"Find whom?" the sultan asked.

"Father, my lizard disappeared by slipping through the grid in the floor where you are standing," Ahmed said. "May I go to Muti? He will help us find him."

"Why not?" the sultan said. "You can always count on Muti to help out. He knows every nook and cranny of the Alhambra. Don't be gone too long. We need to bring David to the Catholic queen."

19

There Is *the* Scary-Looking Man and He Is Right in front of David

⊘

Ahmed and David went on their way, passing a series of corridors and rooms beautifully decorated with arabesques and domes of mocarabes, finally arriving at a smaller room where a dark-haired man dressed in a black robe was standing with his back to Ahmed and David.

"Muti," said Ahmed, "We need you to show us the way to the underground. We have lost Kadar. We saw it go down through a grid in the hall by the harem. Could you please show us the way? I know you know everything about the Alhambra."

Muti, who was looking at a big book, turned around.

David jumped as he recognized the same strange, scary-looking man that had been following the Moorish king and him from the entrance gate through the gardens to the observatory.

Here he was in front of him dressed in a black robe hung over a gray tunic enhanced with a wide leather belt with a precious stone holster holding a gold-studded scimitar, the only bright thing shining about him.

David shook with fear. *Who was this scary, mean-looking man who knew all about the Alhambra?*

David wanted to ask Ahmed about the fierce-looking man, but the man was too close, and David was afraid he would hear. He would have to wait until the man was not in their presence.

Ahmed, on the other hand, seemed undisturbed by the spooky dark man with black, bushy eyebrows, menacing black-as-coal eyes, and a pointed, black beard.

"Of course, Sayyid Ahmed. I'm always at your disposal," the ominous man said. "Is it, however, wise for you to go in the underbelly of the palace, where there are many old and worn-out hot- and cold-water pipes running under the palace, dark pathways, interconnected corridors with dungeons, and storage rooms with a few haunting ghosts of past prisoners and tenants? You could easily get lost or hurt."

"Dungeons and ghosts!" David's eyes lit up. He loved it.

"Can't you come with us?" Ahmed asked, unconcerned about ghosts and the other bad things Muti mentioned.

"I can show you to the basement, but, unfortunately, I need to assist your father, the king, with a meeting in the Hall of the Ambassadors," Muti answered. "Is your father aware of your little adventure to come?"

"Of course, he is," Ahmed answered. "We just left him. He knows I am looking for the blue-green lizard. We were all chasing Axia's bird, Azam, and my lizard. Axia's bird is back in the aviary, but my lizard escaped. Father saw us searching for it everywhere and said you knew everything about the Alhambra."

"Very well, then. Let's go," the scary-looking man said. "I will apprise him of the situation when I meet with him after I return from below ground."

        ᥫᩣ

Without any further questioning, he proceeded outside into the Court of Lion where a forest of columns stood magnificently and proudly showing their extraordinary, minute details of abacuses with carved flowers, leaves, and beautiful calligraphic letters that David did not understand.

David had been in awe the moment he entered the Alhambra. No other castle he had been in so far rivaled the glamorous beauty of the Alhambra. He still was spellbound.

"The columns look like palm trees. How many are there?" David asked.

"One hundred twenty-four," answered the scary-looking man officiously.

They walked through a lush area of green bushes where a striking fountain stood encircled by twelve lions spewing water in very narrow trenches.

"By the way, do you know what the fountain represents?" Muti asked both boys.

"No," answered David, busy looking up at the top of the hundreds of scallops encrusted in the inside of the arches. He suddenly tripped on one of the white marble water channels leading to the marble fountain adorned with twelve lions.

"Oh! No," David shouted, losing his footing and falling backward, almost touching this stunning three-tiered white fountain with water cascading from the top basin.

He fell right into one of the lion's mouths spewing water, and would have gotten all wet if it had not been for Muti grabbing him just in time.

"I guess I need to keep my eyes in front of me and not look up. Thank you, Muti," said David, still unconvinced about the goodness of the odd-looking man.

"The fountain represents the sultan, who showers his loyal and loving subjects with many favors," Ahmed added.

"Exactly," Muti said.

"But why are there twelve lions?" asked David.

"Muti, do you know?" Ahmed asked.

"Could the twelve lions represent the twelve tribes of Israel?" asked David as he continued to examine the fountain's magnificent lions.

"I'm not exactly sure about the meaning of the twelve lions, but I know the history of them," Muti replied. "The lions were taken from a too-powerful Jewish man, Joseph ibn Naghrela, loved by the Berber king he worked for, but disliked by the Muslim people, who killed him because they thought he wanted the throne for himself."

"How sad! How mean to have killed this innocent man because the king loved him!" said David in a low voice. "But look, there is a triangle with a green stone on the forehead of this lion. Do you know what it means?"

"No, I am not sure. Do you?" asked Muti, observing David closely.

"Hmmm," David said. "Could it be the name of a tribe?"

"Possibly," Muti said. "Like I said, all I know is where it came from. You seem to know though, so tell me."

"If the lions belonged to a Jewish man, then I think this one lion could stand for the Levi tribe."

Ahmed had never paid attention to the lions before. He became, however, intrigued by David's interest in the lions. He had been walking by the fountain of lions every day without paying much attention to them. Now he was interested.

"Look, David. This other lion's forehead has a dark-red stone in a triangle. Is that the name of another tribe?" asked Ahmed proudly.

"It must be for the Judas tribe," answered David.

"How come you know so much about the tribes of Israel? Are you—" asked Muti, who was interrupted by Ahmed, who thought he had seen his blue-green lizard.

"David, come," Ahmed said. "I think I see my lizard."

∽

Suddenly, Ahmed left Muti and David and ran toward a door flanked by two more robotic devices.

"Wait for me," David said and hurried after Ahmed. So did Muti.

Ahmed stopped behind a big golden throne, bent down, and said, "Oh! No, it's gone again."

"Do you still want to go underground?" Muti asked. "It seems your lizard is on this floor. It does not look like your lizard went underground."

"It's not here. It disappeared again," said a perky Ahmed ready to go have an adventure and explore the belly of the palace. "I don't see him anymore, but I last saw him by the throne. Where else could he have gone, but down? "

"Let's go down, Sayyid," Muti said, obeying his young master.

Muti approached the back of the massive throne that sat on a tall and colorfully tiled base. He touched a knob and lifted the door up.

"I didn't know there was a door there," Ahmed said surprised to see something that looked like it was part of the throne but was totally inconspicuous.

"It is easy to miss the door," Muti said. "It's behind the throne, and no one ever goes behind the throne."

"But, even if someone went behind the throne, it blends with the throne's design," Ahmed said. "You can't tell at all that this panel rotates to let one enter the underground. Does my father know about this?"

"Yes," Muti said, opening the secret door behind the grand-looking lounging chair that looked like a throne. "Let's go under the Alhambra."

Excited beyond belief, both boys hurried through the open door and descended below ground babbling with joy and wondering what else they would find besides the lizard.

Was it as threatening as Muti had told them?

20

Muti's Warning

෧

They all went down a narrow, poorly lighted spiral staircase that got darker as they got farther down. The stairs ended, and they came to a room.

Muti walked with Ahmed and David into the dimly lit but beautiful room that looked a little bit like the Hall of Ambassadors. Columns encircled the room with a plain fountain at the center. The walls all around the room were decorated with blue, orange, white, and dark tiles decorated with Arabic writing. There were even many scalloped ceiling decorations.

"Wow, we are here," Ahmed said. "We are underneath the palace. I have never been. This is so exciting, and this room looks like the throne room."

"It is," Muti said.

"I am looking forward to this adventure," David said, animatedly.

"This looks like a replica of what is above," Ahmed said. "Why, Muti?"

"This was built in case there is a war and the sultan and his family need to escape," Muti answered. "It was built to make their life down here bearable by duplicating their actual living quarters."

"What else is here?" Ahmed asked, curious.

"Not much else as interesting as this room, but there are cold stone rooms and dirty passageways," Muti said without zeal. "I must get going, Ahmed. Your father is waiting for me. Are you sure you have permission to be here? Are you sure you will be okay here?"

"Yes, I am sure. Again, I do have his permission, and so far, I don't see any problems exploring down here," Ahmed replied. "Underground looks like what we have upstairs, so I will find my way around easily."

"Not quite. There are many corridors. It is a maze down here," Muti said preoccupied. "I don't think your lizard went that far. If you insist on going farther, I would suggest you stay on this path, and it will lead to the exit by the river. Please just walk straight if you decide to hang around here," Muti repeated. "But if I were you, I would go back and not go past this room; I wouldn't stay down here. Believe me, your lizard is probably upstairs and nowhere in these dark corridors."

"But I saw the lizard slip through a grid twice," Ahmed insisted.

"No matter how tempted you are to deviate and follow a different path, don't," Muti warned the boys. "It's dark and confusing down here. There are unseen holes in the ground and untraveled tunnels that could be dangerous. There are also spooky rooms containing many weird things."

Is he telling the truth? thought David, still wondering about the scary-looking man.

Ahmed and David looked at each other as accomplice as if they knew they were, of course, going to deviate from the easy path out.

Muti had caught that accomplice look between the two but said nothing.

"I will hurry back as soon as my duties are done," Muti said. He gave David a very strange look with his dark, penetrating, hellish eyes and left.

David shuddered with fear. *What was that look for?*

All of a sudden, the huge room felt dark, cold, and eerie.

"It looks like a cave down here with rooms built into the stone," David said.

"It does look like a cave to me too. But at the same time, part of it also looks like the Hall of Ambassadors underground," said Ahmed who then asked, "Where should we go first?"

༐

Click. Clank. Clunk. Crack. Click. Clank. Clunk.

Both stopped walking.

"What was that?" asked Ahmed alarmed.

"Who is there?" screamed David.

The noise stopped.

"Probably something or somebody in the Hall above us," Ahmed said, unsure.

"Okay then, let's continue," David said.

"Do you want to go straight and exit by the river, hoping we will see the lizard on the way, or should we go to the left?" Ahmed asked.

"Let's go to the left and explore," David said excitedly. "Are you sure you have never been down here before? What do you think we will find?"

"I have no clue what there is," Ahmed answered. "We are going to leave the palace soon, and the Catholic king and queen are going to take over and oust us out. So I want to see every room of the palace before I go away."

"Do you think there are treasures?" David asked.

"Could be."

༄

Chink, click, clink, clonk, clump was heard again.

"Here are the noises again."

"Weird," David said. "Maybe Muti was right... Do you think we are safe?"

"Sure we are," Ahmed answered. "Muti would not have left us alone. My father trusts him. He did say to stay on the straight path out because of the holes and wells, but we will be careful."

But Ahmed and David did not listen to Muti. They wanted an adventure, and they went off the straight path leaving the twin large hall.

Looking straight ahead to a narrow, dark path with only a few slivers of light in places, Ahmed hesitated for a second and said, "Too boring to just go straight to the end. I want to see what else my father's palace holds. This is my chance."

"I agree," David said. "Look, Ahmed, I see animal footprints. Do you think it is your lizard?"

"Could be," Ahmed said. "Let's follow the track."

Ahmed and David followed the tiny footprints into an unlit corridor with many openings carved into the rock. They could still hear the *clink* and *clunk* though the sounds seemed far away.

ᴄ⁄ᴏ

They entered the first room they saw.

"This must be a storage room for food and drinks," David said, looking at casks and different-sized bins and containers.

"Nothing interesting here," Ahmed said. "And I don't see my lizard anyway. Let's continue."

David was already checking a small room next to the storage room.

"Drat, nothing here either. So far this is kind of boring," David said slightly disenchanted. "Maybe we should just go back."

"Shush," said Ahmed. "Strange, I don't hear anything anymore."

"Hmmm," David said listening. "What do you think it means?"

"I think whatever is making the sound is very close to us or gone."

ᑲ

"Maybe we should lift some of those urns to see if the lizard is underneath."

"Good idea, David."

Ahmed raised the light storage bin with only a few fruits in it. A million brown bugs came out. "No. No Kadar," Ahmed said disappointedly.

Ahmed quickly dropped the urn. "Phew! I'm not touching another one of those again. Who knows what else we will find?"

"Bugs are fun. But look at the wall in the next room, Ahmed," David said thrilled at the prospect of finding something exciting. "I see a little door that's been left open. Let's go see what that's about."

David and Ahmed stepped into the other room and opened the door.

"It looks like a dungeon with an iron-bar door and a slit opening in the wall that lets air and light in."

"It is," Ahmed said, and he went to the unattractive stone bed and shook the straw. "There is fresh straw on it. Someone just slept here."

⁓

"Bingo. Look what I found," he said, pulling a piece of paper with a picture of a map showing some corridors leading to a room with the Arabic words *thahab* and *fidda*.

Ahmed took the yellowed paper and showed it to David.

"What are you so happy about, Ahmed?"

"It is a map," Ahmed said happily. "There is something mysterious about this."

"Let me see it," David said intrigued about the map with the scribbling and lines.

21

Are the Words on the Map Code for Something?

❧

"Weird, the words *thahab* and *fidda* are all over the map," Ahmed said, pointing to the words on the map.

"Do you think they are code for something?" David asked.

"I think they are," Ahmed replied. "They mean *gold* and *silver* in Arabic. Look at the map—it shows the words *gold* and *silver* in this room," he said, pointing to a specific room with the words *fidda* and *thahab* on the map. "Why don't we go there to see if there are thahab and fidda."

"Okay, but it looks complicated to get there, and part of the map is worn out and hardly readable," David said. "Let's sit down for a few minutes and study it before we go look for the gold and silver."

Ahmed and David sat on the cold stone floor scrutinizing attentively the map by the freshly occupied bed.

"There are lots of rooms with marks on them," Ahmed said, studying the map and paying attention to all the details. "We need to go three rooms to the left, then one room to the right, and then the room on the left is the room we are looking for."

"How do we know the map is accurate and shows all the rooms on the way there?" David asked. "If not and there are more rooms, we are going to get lost."

"How many rooms can there be?" Ahmed said, unworried. "We will find our way."

"Is there any other way?"

"Well, I don't know. I have never been here, and I can't tell by the map," Ahmed said.

"Let's look at the map again," David said.

They both pored over the map one more time. But there was no other path marked leading to the gold and silver room except the way Ahmed had already described.

∽

The *chink, clash, clatter, click, clank* noises started again.

Then there was a whimper followed by a *whump* and *whoosh* and then a splash.

"What in the world are those noises we keep hearing?" David asked.

"It sounded like someone complaining or crying as if they were hurt."

"There is also a watery sound," David said, paying attention to the racket heard in the distance.

"We must be close to the river," Ahmed said. "Maybe someone fell in the river?"

"Or may be someone was thrown in the river?" David proposed.

"Or may be something was thrown in the river?" Ahmed suggested, as his imagination filled with a million possibilities.

"Let's go find out," urged David.

Ahmed and David left the old, dingy dungeon cell, went to the left, and counted three rooms as the map indicated. They entered another dark dungeon, but this time the dark dungeon had some slimy green moss growing on the wall.

"Yikes, it smells bad in here," David said, pinching his nose.

"It does. There are droppings all over," Ahmed said. "Let's keep our eyes open for whatever is making that."

"Okay," David said. "I think bats are responsible, and I hate bats. Hey, look—there are bones on the ground."

"Do you think there are human bones in here?" Ahmed asked.

"If there are, no wonder it smells bad here." David said. "Do you think your father or grandfather held prisoners that died here?"

Ahmed wasn't sure how to answer this question, but he did the best he could. "I don't know about my grandfather, but my father is a good and fair ruler and would not want to hurt anyone. He has been a prisoner himself and wouldn't wish any of the misery he suffered on anyone," Ahmed said, walking toward the exit. "Let's leave this gloomy and stinking room."

∽

There was a choice of three doors.

"Three doors," Ahmed said. "Drat! The map does not show three doors."

"That's what I thought; sometimes maps don't show all the details," David said.

Ahmed scratched his head, "That complicates things. What are we going to do?"

"Let's open all three doors and peek in each room," recommended David.

"Good idea," Ahmed said.

David opened the first door. But as he did, a hundred bats whizzed right at him and past him and darted toward Ahmed, who had never seen bats before.

"Yuck," David screamed.

"Shoo, shoo," shouted Ahmed, trying to drive the scary flying mice away. "What are those ugly beasts?"

"They are bats. I dislike them, but they are pretty gentle and intelligent," David said. "Do you know they can eat up to five hundred insects an hour? They do people a service by getting rid of bad insects. The problem is they are scary to look at."

"I have heard of them, but I have never seen one before, and I was told to watch out for them," Ahmed said. "Should we pick up one then and look at it? Do you think it could attack my lizard?"

"Bats are wild animals," David said. "They are not used to people. When they get scared, they bite. And no, they won't attack your lizard. They like moths and beetles."

"There is nothing in this room except a leaking pipe," Ahmed said disappointedly. "I think my lizard is lost."

"And so far we have not seen any wells or holes in the ground like Muti said," David told Ahmed. "Do you think Muti was telling the truth?"

"That's strange, isn't it," Ahmed replied.

❧

Ahmed went to the second room. He opened the door.

"There are pipes going through this room too and two more doors to choose from."

David said, "Come to the third room. That's where I am."

"In a minute," Ahmed answered.

Ahmed went to one door and tried to open it, but it wouldn't budge.

"Maybe you need to come and help me," Ahmed shouted. "This door is stuck, and I want to see what's in the room."

"I'll be right there," David said, checking the room he was in. "Go to the next door."

Ahmed left the stuck door and went to the other door and opened it without a problem.

"Wow! This is unbelievable."

"What? Did you find the treasure room?"

"Nope," Ahmed answered. "There is a stairway that goes way down to a pool of water. I even see boxes with stuff and furniture and..."

⤎

The *click, cluck, clunk, clip, clop* started again.

Then there was a murmur.

"I am convinced there is someone down there," whispered Ahmed, shivering.

Ahmed quickly closed the door and went back to David.

"Very strange," Ahmed said, suddenly extremely curious about who was making this noise. "Why are those people speaking in low voices and sneaking down there with our furniture and boxes of stuff?"

"Do you think they were ordered to move stuff out before the takeover by the Catholic king and queen?"

"I don't know. But if they were told to move stuff out, why are they whispering in low voices?" answered Ahmed suspicious of what was going on. "Do you think my father is aware of people taking stuff?"

"Maybe," David replied. "What do you want to do? Do you want to go down there and spy on them?"

Ahmed thought for a few minutes and replied, "Yes. I'd like to go down there, but first let's find out if there is a treasure room. And if there is, then that's what they are stealing, and it's wrong because it belongs to my family."

"Let's go find out," David said. "But after we leave this room, let's mark all the floors of the rooms we go through with our initials. This will allow us to retrace our steps if we need to come back this way."

David saw a black rock on the ground, picked it up, and said, "I think this will work."

He took the rock and started scratching letters on the ground.

"It works," said Ahmed. "Let's write lots of *A*'s on the ground and *D*'s in a few places. "You are in charge of doing the tracing."

~

"Let's go to the third door," Ahmed said. "According to the map, it leads to the corridor and the treasure room."

They walked to the third room. All the while, David marked the floor.

They opened the third door that led to another room. This room looked much less refined and much more like a cave. They entered it. There was nothing in it except a sweaty, hanging water pipe going through it. The walls were slimy and moldy. There were strange, short tan-colored stalactites hanging from the ceiling too.

"Be careful where you walk," David said, looking around the room to see what had made what looked like piles of shiny, foul-smelling brown rice. He spotted bats hanging in the corner. "You could end up smelling bad."

"What do you think these are?" asked Ahmed as he reached for some of the brown rice.

"These are droppings. Don't touch them, they could be harmful," David said. "Look! There are bats all around here. Who knows, but I have a feeling this is their bathroom!"

"Yuck." Ahmed quickly took his hand away. "What are those things hanging down from the ceiling?" he asked almost touching one.

"Don't touch that either," David said. "Too many bats around here. I think it could be bat pee or something nasty related to bats."

Ahmed got away from the yellow, stinky sites and walked toward the door.

"Now that you mention it," Ahmed said, "it looks like poop hanging down. Thank God you warned me. This place reeks. Let's get out of here."

"I am not sure your lizard came all the way here," David said. "But who knows?"

"I think you are right," Ahmed said. "The lizard is smart and must have gone back upstairs or somewhere nicer."

ҩ

They left the smelly room and followed the map, turning right into a long corridor with openings on both sides.

"Not as easy as the map shows," Ahmed said, looking at the simple map. "It shows to take a left and then take a right. But which opening on the right is the right entrance?"

They both stopped and looked at this long, dark corridor completely confused about which direction to go. They knew they had to go right, but which opening to choose?

"One, two, three, four, five, six, seven, eight, nine, ten," David said, counting more than ten entrances. "Wow! Now where do we go?"

"The walls are carved with words," Ahmed said, examining the wall. "Maybe there is a secret message written on the wall. What do you think?"

"Probably," David said. "But I can't read Arabic."

Ahmed looked at the kufic writing and read the wall carvings, giving up after a few minutes, while David tried to see if there were other clues in the room.

"There are no hints here," Ahmed said. "These are verses from the Koran and poems from Ibn Zamrak. See the line here," he said as he pointed to a series of beautiful signs over the second entrance. "It means, 'Rejoice in good fortune.'"

"Great!" David said, laughing. "That's a good sign we are headed the right way. Look Ahmed, don't the characters above the entrance look like the letters on the map?"

Ahmed looked at the Arabic letters above the entrance and looked at the map to compare them. "I thought you couldn't read Arabic," Ahmed said, grinning. "You are right. They are the same as on the map. The characters mean 'thahab.'"

"Gold," David translated enthusiastically. "We are going to find gold."

"Maybe?"

౭ヘ๑

David was already at the entrance with the gold sign above it. "Come on, Ahmed. Hurry up. Let's go see if the sign is leading us in the right direction."

As Ahmed was about to join David, a sound froze him on the spot.

Sounds of *bump*, *fizzle*, *gargle*, and *gurgle* were audible.

Ahmed said, "David, do you hear that?"

The *gurgle rinky-rink* sound continued and became monotonous even though loud at times. The sound was as if it was part of the rooms they were crossing.

"Come, Ahmed; it is only water going through the pipes," David said authoritatively.

"I think it is more than water...Listen."

The deafening *grumble*, *gurgle*, and *rinky-rink* noises greeted David's ears.

"I'm telling you, Ahmed, it is water going through the pipes," said David, pretending to be sure of himself, when in fact, he was a little spooked.

David did not want to show his fear. Ahmed might panic.

Was it really water going through the pipes?

Was it something else sliding through the pipes? David wearily shrugged his shoulders. *What could he do? Nothing really.*

They could not go back to the main floor of the palace just yet. This was too mysterious and intriguing.

22

A Spider Attacks Ahmed

৵

Everywhere they went underground they heard strange sounds. So what were a few more!

They had not seen much out of the ordinary except bats, bugs, and dried-up old bones—no ghosts, no people, and no gold. So this had to be just a random noise.

"Everything is so echoey down here," David said uneasily. "The sounds bounce back from wall to wall through all the rooms."

Ahmed reluctantly followed David into the cave room with the thahab sign. It had water running from a pipe down the wall.

Ahmed shrieked. "*Heiiiiiiii!*"

David turned around, "What's the matter?"

He didn't say more. He saw Ahmed as white as a sheet. A huge brown spider had landed on Ahmed's nose.

Ahmed was frozen with fear and didn't dare move.

Quickly, David took his little notebook out and whacked the spider off Ahmed's nose. "Ouch!" screamed Ahmed, "Did you have to thump that spider as hard as you did?"

"I'm sorry, Ahmed, but I had to do that," David answered. "It was the spider biting you or me slapping you."

"Did you see the size of that thing?"

"Let's get out of here," David commanded, appraising the delicate situation. "Look at the ceiling. See the little white sacs hanging down? That's where they are coming from. We don't want any more spiders falling on us."

Looking down at the ground to see where the spider had landed, he saw a dark-gray, large-headed salamander with a tail that was as long as its body squirming toward a pile of rocks next to the entrance.

"Look at that—if a salamander can live here, maybe my lizard came here to visit," Ahmed said, laughing and forgetting about the spider.

When they got to the rocks, they saw quite a few salamanders of all sizes leisurely popping their heads in and out of cracks in the rocks.

"No lizard," David said.

"In the last minute, we saw gray salamanders and a brown spider," Ahmed said. "What else do you think we will see?"

"Here is your answer," David replied, showing him a pholcid daddy long legs with giant claws surrounded by a half dozen daddy long legs.

"Do you think the salamanders will attack the spider with their claws?" asked Ahmed fascinated.

As they were bending down to examine more closely, they heard a loud noise like something clashing.

"What was that?" they asked each other as both got back up and looked around.

But there was nothing around them to have caused this noise. All there was were dark, slimy walls crawling with insects: eyeless silverfish, soldier flies, two-pronged bristletails, isopods, woodlouses, and pseudoscorpions.

"Now that's exciting," David said, observing the wall of squirming insects.

"Let's go see what's making this noise," Ahmed said.

☙

They left the daddy long legs and all the bizarre cave insects to go investigate where this new *clatter, clang, bang* noise was coming from.

They very carefully walked straight into another damp, dark room trying to see if the noise was coming from there.

But the noise had stopped.

"Weird!" David said. "Now everything is quiet."

"It seems the noise comes and goes," Ahmed said impatiently. "Will we ever get to the treasure room? There was no gold in that room even though it did have the word *thahab* above the entrance."

"Maybe the word *thahab* means something else besides gold," David said with a wise face. "I think we need to throw the map out and go on our own."

"Look, David, at the worm-like bug with legs. It is blocking our way," Ahmed continued, laughing and looking at the small insect.

"This is a millipede," David answered. "Usually it is brown-black. I think this one is white because there is no light."

David bent down and touched it. The millipede curled up.

"See—it is protecting itself."

"Shush, sh," mumbled Ahmed. "Listen...There it goes again. I hear *whump, whump*, like someone beating something with a heavy object."

Ahmed had walked a few feet ahead of David. Curious, he couldn't wait to see where this passageway would lead and put the map in his pocket. The map had been kind of useless so far.

⁓

The *whump, thump, twack* was getting louder.

Even though he walked slowly, Ahmed slipped; he didn't fall very far, but in his fall, he bumped into a cottony white cloud covering the entrance and part of the room. It was difficult to see.

Trying to keep his balance, his hands struck the gluey white cloud of threads that were covering the whole opening.

"Yuck," said Ahmed softly." What is that? I feel like I put my hands in a giant bowl of honey."

Trying to get the sticky white threads off him, he shook his hands up and down and side to side. It only made matters worse as he walked in the room, clearing the way for David to enter. In the process of squirming and twisting every which way, he became enrobed with the fluffy, white material.

"You look like a white cocoon. No, actually you look more like a mummy," said David seriously. "You did a good job wrapping yourself with spider webs."

"Spider webs!" Ahmed said nervously.

"Yes," David said. "But it's nothing to be concerned about. There don't seem to be any spiders in them."

"You can't be serious," Ahmed said. "What's going to happen to me?"

"Nothing," David said laughing. "Except looking ghoulish."

"You should laugh," Ahmed said. "You should see what's crawling on your shoulder."

David stopped laughing and turned his eyes to his shoulder.

"Eek," said David. "That I don't like. No wonder you never come down here. Things creep up on you every step you take."

"It does seem that way, doesn't it?" Ahmed said, looking around.

"Even though I like bugs, I prefer when they don't surprise me," David added. "I'm sure nothing like this happens up in the palace. There is nothing to harm you up there. Here in this cave, it's another matter. Can you help me and take away this pesky thing away?"

"I am not coming anywhere close to that eight-legged thing with ugly claws," Ahmed said. "Besides, I am having a hard time moving."

"It looks worse than it is," David said. "It is only a fake scorpion. It won't bite you—only me since it's on me. I promise."

"Then if it's fake, why do you want me to take it off your shoulder?" Ahmed replied, examining from a distance this strange bug. "I'm sorry; I won't touch it even if it's a pretend scorpion."

"Oh, don't use your hands," David suggested in frustration. "Just use a stick and brush it off."

"Oh, okay, but it feels weird to move with all the cobwebs sticking to my body," Ahmed said, trying to walk. "Will you help me clean those cobwebs off after I get the scorpion off of you? Do you see any spiders on me?" asked an alarmed Ahmed afraid to move in case there were.

"No. I don't see anything," David answered quietly. "I think the spiders abandoned those webs a long time ago."

Even though all wrapped up, the appeased Ahmed reluctantly picked up a stick with difficulty that was laying at his feet, very carefully lifted off the white scorpion, and batted it away. It flew right through a crevasse in between the stones of the wall.

"Where did it go?" Ahmed asked afraid it landed somewhere on the cocoon wrapping around him.

"Don't worry," David replied. "It's not on you."

"Are you sure?" Ahmed asked.

At this moment, somewhere close by, a voice was clearly heard saying, "Where are we going to take this gold urn?"

"Shush," said David. "Let's go see where the voices are coming from."

They went through a portal, walking in the direction of the voices, not paying any more attention to the grotesque cave crawling with insects, scorpions, millipedes, and spiders. They calmly walked into the next room, Ahmed dressed in white gauze and David just relieved not to have the fake scorpion perched on his shoulder.

23

Ahmed and David's Strategy

❧

They entered a room filled with treasures: gem-encrusted swords, gold trays, ivory-handled knives, bowls, ewers, gold weights, pearl water pipes, emerald flasks, diamond earrings, gold cups, plaques, pen boxes, incense burners, bracelets, head ornaments, mirror cases, goblets, silver lanterns, gold tray stands, blue rock-crystal glass jars, beads, necklaces, pendants, blue and gold bowls, blue ceramic lanterns, gold coins, fans, hangings, royal figures, mirror cases, metal inkwells, emerald daggers, astrolabes, rugs, silver and gold coffers, pearl and ruby necklaces, sabers, and gold, ruby, and emerald rings.

"So, the map was right after all," Ahmed said mystified. "There are treasures, but it looks like my family's treasures."

"Unbelievable. I have seen treasure chests filled with precious stones but nothing like the treasure chests here," said David. "Treasures are everywhere."

David bent down to touch a beautiful dagger encrusted with pearls, emeralds, and rubies, not seeing two dark-skinned men dressed in white *thawbs* tunics with white turbans on their heads come into the room with a chest.

Ahmed touched David's shoulder and in silence pointed to the two engrossed men, who were putting the chest down.

David signaled to Ahmed to go behind a golden door right behind him.

Ahmed quietly snuck behind the golden door. David crawled slowly in between the mounds of gold, silver, and precious objects so as not to attract any attention and joined him.

༄

The two men—one big and one thin—went to another beautifully carved chest and, while laughing, filled it with silver dirhams, copper coins, gold dineros, gold and silver necklaces, diamond rings, golden lanterns, and fans with red silk tassels.

"How much do you think the silver dirhams are worth?"

"Millions."

"How about the gold coins?" the other man asked.

"Just as much."

"We are going to be rich," the two thieves bragged. "And to think Muhammad the 12th is trusting us to take these out of the Alhambra and bring all his possessions to Morocco."

"He is a good person but too trusting," the thin man said.

"You know what? He will never leave Spain," the heavyset man said. "Worse, the Catholic monarchs will confiscate all of his belongings when they take over. He trusts them, and he should not because once Muhammad the 12th surrenders the Alhambra, he is done. They will take all the gold and silver from him and use them to fund Columbus's upcoming explorations of a new world. So, we might as well cooperate with him and let him think that we will safeguard his treasures."

"And we will, won't we?" the thin man said unsure if he should believe his accomplice.

"Yes, but don't you see if he does not leave Spain, the treasures will be ours," the heavyset man said, smiling confidently; in his mind he was already building himself a palace in Morocco.

"Are you sure the Catholic monarchs will fund Columbus's travels?" the thin man asked.

"That's what the gossip is," the bulky man said. "Queen Isabella is for Columbus and Ferdinand is against, but he is getting closer to agreeing."

The two men finished filling the golden chest and scanned the place rich with the king of Granada's possessions.

"Are we ready to go down to the river?" the thin man asked.

"Yes," the portly man answered. "Let's hurry and get there before Muti gets here. He will want to inventory every item."

"Can he be trusted?" the thin man asked. "Maybe he wants the sultan's gold for himself as much as we do."

"I don't trust him," the burly man answered.

❦

Ahmed was growing more and more upset and whispered to David, "I can't believe Muti is in on it. I need to go and warn my father. His trusted men are pilfering all our stuff. I just can't believe it."

I can, thought David.

Ahmed was so disturbed about these dishonest men's plans that he forgot how uncomfortable he was wrapped in white cottony spider webs looking like a mummy.

David said, "Do you believe they are taking the gold and silver on orders of your father? Shall we follow them? This way we can tell your father where the thieves have taken the stuff."

"Yes, let's do that. I can't wait to ask my father if he ordered them to take our possessions to Morocco. I don't believe he did," Ahmed said convinced his father wouldn't act in secret. "He will want to put a stop to that. These men are thieves. How can people think they can steal and get away with it?"

❦

As he was leaving, the scraggy man picked up a few gold coins and quickly slipped them in his pocket, but in his haste, a few escaped and fell down with a *ting a ling* sound.

The other bulky man turned around and angrily said, "Trying to sneak coins behind my back, huh?"

"What harm can a few coins do? There are plenty for both of us," the scrawny coin thief answered, showing no remorse. "Watch where you are going, or we will both roll all the way down to the Darro River."

The stout man shrugged his shoulders and took a few coins too.

Ahmed said, "Did you see that? I just can't believe it. These are my family's coins. He is putting coins in his pocket as if they were his. I just want to go there and punch him; I'm so mad."

"You mean you want to punch both of them," David said.

"I want to, but I can't," Ahmed answered sadly. "I'm just a kid. My father will have to take care of them."

"There is so much here," the obsessed man said. "We need to come right back and load up some more. I like some of those weapons lying on top of the jewelry."

Both robbers furtively left the room carrying the chest filled with precious jewels and gold and silver coins.

⁓

"Shall we wait here?" Ahmed asked nervously. "They are coming back."

"Do you think they are coming back for these spectacular knives?" David asked, pointing at the sharp knives decorated with fancy stones.

"Probably," Ahmed answered. "These knives are very old, valuable family daggers. This one dagger is my father's favorite."

Ahmed picked one among many and gave it to David.

"Look at the handle," Ahmed said. "Its gold hilt is set with huge green emeralds, diamonds, and rubies. It's protected by a gold sheath that is covered with fifty Indian diamonds."

David removed the sheath and examined the Indian diamonds closely.

"The cover is as beautiful as the dagger itself. No wonder people want to steal objects like these," David said. "Has your father ever used it?"

"No, my father is a man of peace. It was given to him by a Turkish sultan at my birth."

Ahmed continued, "I am taking the dagger away from here. I will return this dagger to my father. It belongs to him, and he should keep it close."

David gave the priceless gold and diamond dagger back to Ahmed.

Ahmed put the precious dagger in his pocket.

"I don't understand why all these items of great value are here," Ahmed said, shaking his head in disbelief.

"There are some great things here," David said softly.

"All I can figure out is that my father is getting ready to turn the Alhambra over to the Catholics. But what I don't understand is why these men seem to be happy taking our belongings. It is enough he is losing paradise. Does everyone need to take everything away from him?"

"I feel bad for your family," David said. "Maybe you can help by letting your father know what is going on. In the meantime, let's go see where they went."

"David, I want you to have a few silver dirhams. You are more deserving than anyone I know. As the son of the sultan, I can do that," Ahmed said.

He bent down and picked up a few silver coins and gave them to David.

૨૭

They hurried toward the exit of the treasure room, passing by more priceless jewelry.

"I recognize my mother's exquisite silver and gold bracelets and..."

He did not finish.

"Abdul. Abdul. Where are you?" screamed an uptight voice.

"Oh! Oh, it is Muti," said Ahmed shakily, not sure what Muti was all about. "Muti must think we left. I don't want him to see us. What do you think?"

"I agree," David said.

❧

They rushed to the opening of the next room. There was a small landing with hundreds of steps.

"Kind of scary," said Ahmed. "It goes down a long way. You can't even see the end."

"Do you think the thieves went this way?" David asked.

"I think so."

"Is it the way that Muti told us to take?" David asked

"I am not sure," Ahmed answered. "We went in so many directions."

"Maybe all paths end up here," David said.

"I don't think so, even though this does seem to go to the river," Ahmed said. "Why would Muti tell us to use this way if he knew the thieves would be here?"

"Maybe he didn't," David said. "And maybe there are many ways to the river."

"Look at this—it's definitely not the way Muti told us to take. Muti told us to go through what looked like a straight corridor. And this was off the path he told us about. This looks like a path that nobody knows about but a few," Ahmed said, pointing at the mysterious-looking stepped tunnel. "I heard my father's guards talking to him about a secret route. I'm wondering if this is the one. Hmmm, do you think my father has been here or even knows where this escape route is?"

"At some point, he would have had to learn that there were ways to escape without being caught," David suggested as if he were an expert.

୧୬

"I see the two men," Ahmed said excitedly in a low voice. "They stopped halfway. Let's spook them."

The two men were close enough to be heard.

"This chest is heavy," the thin man said. "Why did you have to fill it up?"

Ahmed took a dirham and threw it at them and knelt down so the thieves would not see them.

The silver coin hit a wall of bats and bounced back on the heavyset man's head.

"What are you doing?" he yelled. "Throwing things at me?"

"Calm down," the thin man said. "How could I? I'm holding the chest just as you are. Maybe it is Muti?"

୧୬

Just then, a cloud of bats appeared, batting their wings vigorously in the two men's faces. As they were standing on one of the many steps, they couldn't see anything and were afraid to lose their balance.

The men started jumping up and down to scare the bats away, unwilling to let go of the chest and were thus unable to chase the disoriented bats that persisted in hanging around them, looking for insects and protecting their territory.

Ahmed decided to throw another coin.

"Ouch!" screamed the thin man. "You are getting back at me. Where did you get the coin? It looks like I am not the only one who borrowed a few coins."

"I didn't..." the other man said, not finishing because a voice boomed loud and clear.

"Abdul, where are you? I have been looking for you," screamed an irate voice. "Please say something. I have an urgent matter to discuss with you."

One of the men said sternly, "Don't make any noise. He will hear us and come find us. We don't want that just yet. So be *quiet!*"

"How can I be quiet when bats are attacking us as if we were food?" replied the nervous man.

"What urgent matter could he be talking about?" the heavyset man snickered. "I don't trust Muti."

Ahmed said, "Let's throw more coins and make noise. I want Muti to come and find these thieves."

◕◞

"Isn't he a thief too?"

"By the looks of it, he seems to be," Ahmed replied.

Just then the thin man, who was very superstitious, looked up and saw this funny white wrapped-up form coming down toward them. He couldn't keep his calm any longer and let go of the chest screaming and running.

The gold chest hit the wall with a *clatter, clack, crick, crack, smack*.

"You fool," the heavyset man shouted. "What have you done? Half the chest's contents are on the steps now."

The scared thin man didn't care, and he left the heavyset man with the gold coins and the jewels spread all over the steps as he ran down as fast as he could.

"Now what are you doing leaving me alone with stuff everywhere?" yelled the furious, heavyset man. "Where are you going? Come back here and help me put this stuff back in the chest, or I'll tell on you!"

But the shaken little man could not get away fast enough. To see a white ghost was a bad omen, and he wanted no part of it.

24

Is There a Jinn in the Secret Escape Route?

༄

Ahmed thrilled to see the stupefied reaction of the thin man and was hoping for a repeat for the heavyset one. He continued his ghastly walk down followed by David, who decided to add noise to the nightmarish spectacle.

Following Ahmed, David took a silver coin out of his pocket and scraped it on the rock wall, making a *vzzzt* sound as they walked down toward the heavyset man.

The heavyset man was not deterred by the macabre appearance of the white form walking toward him to a metallic sound. He was more interested in recovering the treasures as he calmly bent down to quickly grab the invaluable objects and return them to the banged-up golden chest.

"Is the man blind? Why is he continuing as if nothing were happening?" whispered the white figure.

The *clang clack gr gr k k grk* of the coin scratching the wall and the soft whisper had become a weird, vibrating echo bouncing on the dark walls and sliding down the whole tunnel.

The unconcerned heavyset man continued picking up the spilled priceless objects but was slowing his pace.

"What is this racket all of a sudden?" mumbled the heavyset man grumpily as he finally put the last piece back in the damaged golden chest.

As the echo got louder, he slowly got up and looked around with fear in his eyes. Then he saw a precarious white ghost coming at him.

"A jinn," he said, trembling and not taking the time to really observe the noisy white ghost.

He picked up the heavy chest and awkwardly but with superhuman strength walked down as fast as he could.

Ahmed and David were only a few steps behind the sweaty man holding the big chest of stolen treasures who, in his haste, never looked back to see what was following him.

℘

Then a *kata-kata* and *gwuf gwuf* sound was heard.

Footsteps followed.

"There you are. I have been calling Abdul, but he did not answer. Where is he?" Muti asked.

The petrified thin man just whizzed past the sinister-looking man and tripped over the man's feet. In his stumble, the stolen gold and silver coins came out of his pocket, spilling like milk at the foot of the evil-looking man.

"What is this, Abaan?" screamed the outraged dark-haired man. "Are you taking profits and not sharing with me? Is Abdul doing the same? Wait till I get a hold of him."

Abaan had had enough. *There was a jinn about.* Without responding or stopping, he ran toward the exit of the tunnel. He was scared of both the angry man and the white ghost.

"Abdul, Abdul, come out immediately and meet with me," yelled the displeased man. "Come and pick up these coins that fell out of Abaan's pocket!"

"What is wrong with Abaan?" the raging man shouted.

Abdul heard the aggravated voice of Muti and stopped on his descent, unsure of what to do next. Looking for another way out, he looked behind him. *What's that?* thought the thief. *I am not dreaming. This is a jinn.*

The white jinn was getting closer. He closed his eyes and said a prayer, asking God to remove the jinn from his presence. He reopened his eyes, hoping the white jinn had disappeared, but the white jinn was still there coming toward him.

"Which way should I go?" murmured the sweaty, heavy man to himself. *If I go down, I face a furious Muti. If I go up, I deal with a jinn. Which one do I want to deal with? A spirit or a man?*

ᥱᕽ

Ahmed was afraid to talk because his voice would become a human echo, but David continued scratching the wall with his silver coin.

Ahmed wanted to whisper in David's ear so he stopped walking abruptly.

David bumped into him, dropping the silver coin that went *ding, jingle, jangle* all the way down to Abdul.

"Abdul, I heard that," the man screamed. "What was that noise? What are you doing?"

Abdul was shaking with fear and didn't move. He didn't answer. He didn't dare look at the coin that had come to rest on the tip of his shoe.

"I know you are there," said the irritated man. "I'm coming up."

Taking his courage in both hands, Abdul put the heavy chest down and shouted, "I'm coming down. I need to look for Abaan, who ran away scared of a white ghost." He actually had no intention of looking for Abaan.

Forgetting all about the coin resting on his shoe, Abdul began walking and sent the coin vaulting ten feet up before landing back on a stair. The coin immediately started rolling down, making *ding, clink, clank* sounds every time it hit part of the rock stairs.

Abdul was hoping Muti wouldn't come up to meet him. He would come back later to fetch his precious cargo.

~~

Ahmed whispered to David, "What do you want to do? Stay here or go down?"

This time there was no echo.

"Let's go where the treasure chest is," answered David softly.

They walked down noiselessly to the deserted treasure chest.

"Let's stay here a minute and see what happens when Abdul gets down to where Muti is," whispered David.

"This cobweb is starting to itch badly," said a wriggling Ahmed. "I have been wrapped in this far too long."

"You want me to take it off of you now?" asked David quietly.

"Would you?"

David picked up a golden dagger encrusted with diamonds from the precious treasure chest and with it started peeling the cobweb off Ahmed.

"You have style," laughed Ahmed, looking at the magnificent golden dagger that David was using to scrape the white blanket off him.

"A prince deserves the best," replied a laughing David.

David removed the thick white cloud carefully and noticed, to his horror, that little cotton-ball cocoons that were part of the spider web were on Ahmed's back.

Hmmm, he thought. *Are there spiders in the cocoon waiting to hatch?*

David stayed quiet about them. He preferred not to say anything to Ahmed, who would panic if he knew.

Cautiously, he took the rest of the spider web off Ahmed, hoping none of the baby spiders would come out of the little cocoons.

"Finally, I can breathe easily," said Ahmed with a sigh of relief.

"So can I," answered a thankful David, checking to make sure no cotton ball had somehow found its way onto his back.

"Abdul must be with Muti. Listen..." said Ahmed. "They are talking. Can you hear what they are saying?"

"No," David answered. "Let's get closer."

25

Is Muti a Thief?

⁓

Ahmed, freed from his cocoon and finally looking normal, and David, anxious to get out of the Alhambra's underground caves, ventured down at a very cautious pace. They paid attention to every noise. Both were afraid of coming face to face with the two barbarous men.

Their voices became clearer.

"Did you see two kids around?" the nervous, mean-looking man said. "I tried to tell them that it was dangerous to go explore the tunnels and rooms under the Alhambra, but they insisted. The son of the sultan lost his lizard and saw it go down an opening in the floor. He was determined to go find it. Did you see them?"

"No, Muti," answered Abdul. "What was the urgent matter you wanted to talk to us about?"

Muti didn't have a chance to respond.

⁓

Klopp klopp klopp.

"Ahmed, do you hear the *klopp klopp*?" David mumbled.

"It's a horse," Ahmed whispered back. "We must be very close to the end of the tunnel."

"Muti, are you in there?" boomed a new voice loudly.

"It's my father," said a surprised Ahmed. "What is he doing here?"

"Sounds so loud," David said softly. "He is not alone. It sounds like there are a few people with him."

"I am here, Your Majesty," Muti answered very calmly and politely.

"Have you seen the children yet?" Muhammad XII asked distressed. "I'm concerned. They have been gone a long time."

Caught off guard, Ahmed and David looked at each other.

"What's going to happen if we say we are here?" Ahmed asked David.

"Muti will know we have heard him talking about the treasure," David answered.

"That's what I am afraid of," Ahmed whispered.

"Don't worry," David said. "Your father will protect you, I'm sure."

"Why don't we act as if we just got here? Talk loudly and pretend we haven't seen or heard anything?" Ahmed said.

"What about the treasure box on the steps?" David asked.

"Hmmm," Ahmed replied. "Let's pretend we have just found it."

"Okay."

Making a lot of noise, laughing, and talking, Ahmed and David came down the steps.

"Ahmed, I hear your voice. Is that you, child?" the relieved sultan said.

"Father?" Ahmed asked. "Is that you down there?"

"I was concerned when you and David did not come back up to the Hall of Ambassadors," the sultan replied. "Come down. I'm waiting for you."

"We will be right there," screamed Ahmed excitedly.

Muti and Abdul looked at each other in dismay, afraid they would be found out.

೧

Ahmed and David arrived at the bottom of the steps out of breath.

"I'm so glad to see you, Father," Ahmed said, running to his father. "We saw one lizard, but it was not Kadar. Unfortunately, our search was useless. Maybe you can come with me and look. We were afraid to lose our way. All we saw were a million bugs."

Ahmed went to his father and gave him a big hug. "David likes bugs, but I don't," Ahmed said. "Father, there are so many rooms around here.

Can you take me to them and explore them with us? Muti could be our guide."

Muti became uncomfortable when he heard Ahmed's demands.

"I'm not sure I have time just now," the sultan answered, ignorant of everything that had just happened.

"Please, Father. It would be so much fun to explore with you."

"What do you think, Muti?" the sultan asked. "Would you accompany us?"

"I'm not sure it is a good idea, Your Majesty," Muti answered, sweating profusely. "Lots of bad smells, bugs, and holes."

"And lots of bats," added Abdul, who wanted to dissuade the sultan from going into the underground rooms, afraid the sultan would find some of the treasures already gone.

As Abdul was talking, David whispered in Ahmed's ear, "These two don't want to see your father and you close to the treasure room. Very suspicious. They moved the treasures without his knowledge."

"Father, why don't we go now that you are here," Ahmed implored decisively.

"Muti, it would please my son; are you ready?"

"If Your Majesty wishes...But just to remind His Majesty, you do have a meeting scheduled in forty minutes. A meeting that was changed once already because you mentioned having to return David to the Catholic monarchs," Muti said. "But definitely after your meeting, I will gladly guide you through the underground rooms and tunnels unless it is imperative we go now."

The sultan agreed. "Let's wait until after the meeting."

৩৯

Abdul was fidgeting nervously. He had cheated both Muti and the sultan. He would put the blame on this little blond-haired foreigner for the damaged golden chest full of irreplaceable treasures laying halfway down the stairway. He would tell Muti that Abaan and he came to investigate the noise and found this white jinn on the stairs.

"Abdul, is everything okay?" Muti asked.

"Yes," Abdul answered nervously.

৩৯

"Look, Father. There are coins on the ground. Did you drop them?" Ahmed asked as he bent down to collect the dozen or so silver and gold coins scattered around a very jumpy Abdul and a pretending-to-be-calm Muti.

"No, it is the first time I've see them," the sultan answered with a frown on his face. "Muti, what do you know of those?"

Muti didn't answer. He was busy looking at Abdul, David, and Ahmed.

"David, help me. How do you think these coins got here?" Ahmed said loud enough for his father to hear, winking at his partner in good deeds.

"Strange," David replied, wanting to reinforce Ahmed's questioning reaction.

Ahmed and David picked up the dozen or so coins under the silent glances of the sultan, Muti, and Abdul. David gave his coins to Ahmed. Both children remained mum about the deserted treasure chest sitting on the steps behind them.

ℰↄ

"Muti, do you know anything about these coins being here?" the sultan repeated.

"No, Your Majesty, but I will certainly investigate as soon as possible and will let you know as soon as I find out," Muti said, looking at the sultan and Abdul.

"Father, can David have a few coins?"

"Yes."

Ahmed gave the collected coins to the sultan, his father, but he forgot all about the dagger in his pocket.

The handsome young sultan then took a few coins and gave them to David.

"David, it has been a pleasure sharing the Alhambra with you. May you bring back some great memories of the palace and of our family," the sultan said. "Here is another souvenir of your time spent here."

David graciously accepted the silver and gold coins and looked at them for a minute. They were more beautiful than the ones he had picked and used to scratch the wall.

"Thank you, Sultan. It has been so much fun visiting the Alhambra with you and exploring it with Ahmed," David said. "I hope to be able to come back one day soon."

Still on his horse, the young sultan said, "We would love to see you back. Now, let's bring you to the Catholic monarchs."

"Ahmed, would you like to come with us? We will look for the little white donkey with the blue eyes on our way back. I'm sure it is close by."

"Yes, Father," Ahmed answered. "I would love to come with."

"Muti, could you mount Ahmed in front of me and David behind me?" the sultan asked. "I will take both with me to the Catholic monarchs."

"As you wish, Your Majesty," said Muti. "Are you sure you don't need us to escort you?"

"I'm sure," the sultan said.

Muti placed Ahmed on the horse, and Abdul helped David get on and sit comfortably.

"Okay, children, I hope this is not too uncomfortable," the sultan said. "It is only a short ride from here. We will be there in the blink of an eye."

26

David Says Good-bye

to the Alhambra

❧

Quietly, the horse walked slowly out of the tunnel into the green and lush field by the singing blue river.

David sadly turned around to look at the beautiful, dreamlike Alhambra and saw Muti strike Abdul's face hard.

David poked Ahmed and whispered, "Look at Muti. He is pretty hard on Abdul."

Ahmed saw Muti's angry behavior. He knew Abdul had been wrong in stealing but didn't think he deserved being slapped around by Muti. Muti was just as bad, and it was up to his father, not Muti, to inflict a punishment.

After a few minutes of hesitation, Ahmed said, "Father, are we taking all of our possessions with us when we leave the Alhambra?"

"Of course we are," answered the sultan. "Why do you ask?"

"Is Muti in charge of the moving?" Ahmed asked.

"So many questions, Son. Why?"

"Well, strangely enough, David and I came across some sort of storage room filled with all kinds of valuable objects."

"Such as?" the sultan asked.

"So many things....Jewelry, rugs, hangings, daggers, and golden chests of coins," Ahmed answered. "And I think Muti and other servants were taking them to the river. I heard them say you ordered them to move our things to Morocco. Did you know, Father, that they were taking our things to the river?"

"Hmmm, when we get back, you and I—under Muti's guidance—will go to that storage room and see exactly what is going on there," the sultan answered as best as he could. "Unfortunately, we must face the eventuality of leaving and taking our possessions with us."

"Father, do we need to tell Muti and take him with us?" Ahmed asked nervously, changing his mind about having Muti as a guide. "Is there someone else who can escort us through the many rooms of the underground?"

"Why not Muti? He knows the underground better than anyone else." He paused and then added, "Let me think of who else."

"Thank you, Father," Ahmed replied.

But the king's previously calm face became preoccupied. He was wondering why Ahmed didn't want to have Muti as their guide.

⌒

"Oh! Look, Father, I see the little white donkey with the blue eyes resting under a tree."

The sultan looked and saw the little blue-eyed donkey all alone and said, "Ahmed, why don't I let you off here, and you take the little blue-eyed donkey back home. This way we won't lose it again, and everyone will be happy to have him back."

Ahmed wanted to obey but was afraid to go back alone in case he'd run into Muti. He was now afraid of Muti.

"Father, I'm sure the blue-eyed donkey will be here when we come back, and I really want to go with you to meet the Catholic monarchs."

The sultan ignored Ahmed's request. He expected to be obeyed without question.

Ahmed didn't persist.

⌒

They approached the tree where the little blue-eyed donkey was standing with Jamal the Handsome and Latif the Gentle.

"Oh, good! I'm glad you two are here," the sultan told his guards. "You will bring the little donkey back to the Alhambra immediately and make sure my daughter and wife see it. They have been waiting anxiously for news of it. They will be pleased to have it back. Come and see me later, and you will be rewarded. By the way, have you been in the underground of the Alhambra?"

Ahmed smiled, hoping his father would now let him go meet the Catholic monarchs.

Jamal the Handsome and Latif the Gentle looked at each other uncertain about telling the truth to their beloved, kind, but unlucky sultan. They knew all about the different rooms and tunnels under the Alhambra. They used to play hide and seek when they were younger until Muti put a stop to anyone going under the Alhambra unless they had his permission.

Instead of answering the question directly, Latif the Gentle said, "Your Majesty, we are obedient servants and follow orders. Very few are allowed under the Alhambra. But we know of someone who knows every nook and cranny."

Latif and Jamal were dying to know why the sultan wanted to know but remained silent since they would find out soon enough. Everyone knew what was going on at the Alhambra almost all the time.

"Please make sure you come and see me later with the name of that person," the pensive king said. "I will be in the Hall of Ambassadors."

"Will Muti be there?" Jamal asked nonchalantly.

"Yes," the sultan answered, now wondering why Jamal was also concerned about Muti's being there.

"Can we meet you privately at a later time?" Jamal asked the sultan. "We need to keep the name of the person secret. We don't want him to be in trouble, and he could be for knowing. Even Muti cannot know, Your Majesty. "

"We were told to keep watch over the Gates of Arms right now," Latif said. "But if Your Majesty wants us there at the same time as Muti, we will be there."

"I understand you have a job to do," the sultan replied. "We will have a private audience held only with the both of you and I later, after your watch."

"And me, Father," Ahmed begged.

"Of course, Son," the smiling sultan said.

"You are both dismissed," the sultan said. "Please bring the donkey back to the Alhambra."

"At your service," the two guards answered politely and took the little donkey on the path to the Alhambra.

ᴄ⁄ᴏ

Turning to Ahmed the sultan fretfully asked, "Are you sure you want to come with me and see the queen and king of Spain? These are difficult times for the Moors."

"Yes, Father," Ahmed said.

"We are still negotiating the conditions of the surrender. Who knows what they will do when they see both of us on their encampment. They might demand a ransom," the sultan said worriedly. "I am very hesitant about your accompanying me...They might want to keep you as a hostage to expedite the surrender," continued the worried sultan.

"Father, I'm going to be king one day. I have seen you, and like you, have lived many harrowing moments, and we have survived. It would not be the first time we are held prisoners. If the Catholic monarchs want to keep me to make sure you do surrender, I'm sure they will treat me as one of them. I'm still a child, and they would not mistreat me; don't you agree?" said Ahmed naïvely, trying to be wise beyond his years.

"Nevertheless, I will make sure nothing happens to you," he said, hugging his son tenderly. "And to achieve that, we will just drop David at a safe distance from the monarch's new residence in Santa Fe. I will not go close so as to create a new situation," said the pensive sultan Muhammad XII.

Unfortunately, how much power do I still have? thought the sad and defeated king of Granada.

All three watched in silence as the sweet little white donkey was led up to the Alhambra. However, the last sultan of Granada was worried—not about the donkey, but about his family's welfare.

⁓

They, in turn, started walking toward the Catholic monarchs' tents in the village of Santa Fe. Passing groves of sweetly scented oranges trees; glorious red pomegranates trees; tall and short green trees; and yellow, pink, and purple flowers everywhere, the sultan had tears in his eyes knowing that soon this magnificent earthly paradise would be no longer be his.

Ahmed felt his father's torment, "That's okay, Father," Ahmed told his forlorn father. "We might lose the Alhambra, but will be together as a family, and we will create another kingdom."

"Yes, my wise Son, we will," said a smiling sultan, knowing it was not easy to have a kingdom, much less create one; but he kept his thoughts to himself.

❧

"Oh! I see red and yellow tents and lots of flags flying on top of buildings," said the excited David. "Is that where we are going?"

"Yes," replied the cheerless king of Granada.

They arrived at Santa Fe by a small, lonely alley where not one person was seen. The proud king knew the area around the Alhambra well, and he had purposely chosen a safe path out of the public eye.

Everything was quiet except for the busy chirping of a few birds.

"David, for safety reasons, I must leave you at the entrance to town," the uncomfortable sultan said. "You can easily ask anyone for directions to the queen's quarters. It is a very small town, so you won't have any problem finding someone to help you."

"I don't see anyone. Where is everyone?" asked a fearful David, wondering if Columbus was really there. "Maybe Columbus left?"

Then David remembered. *Oh well! If he is not, I still have my coin,* thought David, regaining his confidence.

"I'm sure Columbus would not leave without you," the Moorish king of Granada answered. "Don't worry, we will see someone soon."

෴

But as they advanced, there still was no one in sight.

The sultan decided he could not leave a young boy unfamiliar with the surroundings alone. He felt responsible for his welfare and his safety though he had a bad feeling about this. *What would the Catholic queen and king think about him being in their town at this moment? Was he putting his son in jeopardy?*

"We must get closer," the king of Granada said. "I don't want to leave you here by yourself. You could get in harm's way. Does Columbus know for sure where you are?"

"I'm not sure if he knows I'm here," David answered. "I found myself alone in the middle of town where I met the princesses of Castile."

"Then I'm sure the princesses told their mother, who in turn must have said something to

Columbus," the sultan said. "Don't worry, David. The question is, where do I drop you off? I'm not sure I want to see the queen of Spain."

Ahmed was not saying a word. It was as if he felt something out of the ordinary was going to happen to him.

Reluctantly but bravely, the king of Granada continued on the path to Santa Fe village in the direction of Queen Isabella's quarters.

27

Joanna's Unexpected Invitation to the Moor Shocks Her Friends

~

A young girl's voice was suddenly heard saying, "You are *it*."

Then lots of young people, some twenty kids, came out of hiding, laughing and pointing to a vivacious young girl. "I told you to come with me, Maria, but as usual, you wanted to do your own thing. Now you are *it*."

"What's wrong with being *it*? I like it when people look for me," said the merry Maria, throwing the apple she was eating at the sultan's horse that she did not see.

"Yes, we know," answered the eldest, attentive Joanna sarcastically.

The surprised sultan's horse jerked and almost threw off his distinguished cavalier while uttering a series of snorting neighs.

"Whoa, wo," said the sultan, pulling quickly but gently on the horse's reins and stabilizing the nervous horse.

"Look who is here?" shouted the beautiful, perky Princess Maria.

"David!" answered the astonished twelve-year-old Princess Joanna.

"We lost you way back," Maria said.

"Where did you go?" Joanna asked. "Columbus was looking for you. He will be glad to see you."

"I'll be happy to see him too," David said. "I got stuck behind some donkeys when I found a white baby donkey. Then I looked for you, but you were gone, and bulls were coming at me."

"Bulls coming at you," Catarina said. "Scary. You are very brave."

"But the sultan saved me and took me to the Alhambra that was close by, where I saw all kinds of unbelievable contraptions," David answered. "Now the sultan was good enough to bring me here safely. He thought I had had my share of strange adventures to venture here alone."

The princesses and their entourage became quiet, stopped their games of hide and seek, and gathered around David and the sultan. They were caught off guard by the presence of their enemy in front of them. But, at the same time, they were captivated by the little man with a white turban on his head dressed all in white, whom they had been told was their enemy. They examined the handsome young sultan with curiosity. They had heard of the exotic young sultan but had never seen him close. All of a sudden, they realized that the sultan didn't look like an enemy but seemed like them, but with a different appearance.

The children knew people were celebrating the upcoming surrender of the sultan, but they had imagined him to be a mean-looking man. Instead, they found him handsome and mysterious looking.

∽

Joanna was the most daring of the group and, to the dismay of her group of young friends, she went to the sultan saying, "Hello, I'm Princess Joanna. Welcome to Santa Fe."

"Joanna, what are you doing talking to the Moor?" her young friend Francisco Fernandez de la Vega asked loud enough for the sultan to hear.

"Why not? He is a person just like you and me," the princess said kindly. "May I take you to my mother, Queen Isabella of Spain?" she continued compassionately, not caring what her friends thought of her actions, knowing it was the right thing to do even if the sultan was an enemy. "Doesn't the prayer book say, 'Love your enemies'?"

The exotic-looking king of Granada looked at the charming young princess. "That's very gracious of you, but I'm not sure the feeling will be mutual. I am not sure your parents will feel as warmhearted as you do," the young man said politely. "And I must get back to the Alhambra as I have people waiting to discuss matters of state. But would you be kind enough to escort our young guest, David, to your distinguished parents, the queen and king of Spain?"

"Certainly," replied the kindhearted twelve-year-old princess.

David eagerly jumped off the sultan's horse. He couldn't wait to tell Columbus about his experience with the sultan at the Alhambra.

Ahmed was quietly observing the young crowd with as much curiosity as they had about him and his father.

"Good-bye, Sultan," David said sadly. "I enjoyed spending time with you and Ahmed at the Alhambra. Hope to see you again sometime."

"Good-bye, young David," the sultan said. "Remember our palace of joy and beauty. May Allah be with you always."

"Good-bye, David," Ahmed said. "I hope you find a lizard and name it Kadar."

"I will do that. I hope you find yours," David said. "I had fun exploring the Alhambra with you."

"Me too," Ahmed said.

Joanna smiled at the kind sultan, quickly hooked her arm in David's, led him away from the sultan, and walked toward the building decorated with a hundred Spanish flags.

David turned back one more time to look at his special friends riding toward the magical red Alhambra.

As soon as Carlos Jimenez de Cisneros, one of the teens, saw the sultan, he ran to the queen's quarters. He had found her in prayer in the stunning chapel. She immediately interrupted her contemplation when she found out the Moorish king was on their grounds.

28

Will the Sultan Agree

to Snack with the Queen

of Spain?

℘

The queen left the chapel promptly, followed by a few men, one of whom was Christopher Columbus. They walked rapidly toward the entrance of the garden where the sultan had first appeared and was now leaving.

"Sultan Muhammad," shouted Queen Isabella in a loud but sympathetic voice that carried the sounds all the way to the sultan, who had not gone very far from where he had left David.

The sultan heard the queen's voice. He stopped without looking back, hesitated, and then came back halfheartedly to meet the beautiful, dictatorial Spanish queen, who was smiling at him gently.

"Greetings, Queen Isabella," said the noble king of Granada. He didn't have it in his heart to be friendly with the queen who had just manipulated the surrender of Granada, but he nevertheless remained courteous. "I have brought back a young guest of yours. I found him being chased by the running bulls. Apparently he saved your daughters from a perilous situation in the middle of town."

The queen, who was not aware of her daughters' escapades, threw a concerned look at her daughters, who in turn lowered their eyes in shame for hiding the truth from her.

"Daughters, when did this happen?" asked Queen Isabella gravely. "I will need to know more about this. However, this will have to wait till after my visit with the sultan."

Queen Isabella had at the moment a very important guest to deal with, an unusual guest who was still in possession of the Alhambra.

Continuing in a calmer tone, she added, "Sultan Muhammad, may I show my gratitude for rescuing our guest, Columbus's precious friend, by inviting you to join us for some *tapas* and *jerez*?"

"Your Majesty is very kind, but my council is waiting for me back at the Alhambra," the uncomfortable king of Granada answered. "I'm afraid I must decline."

"Oh! Sultan you are here now. Join me if only for a few minutes," the imposing queen of Spain insisted. "I assure you this will be a friendly *merienda*, and no politics will be discussed."

The young king of Granada looked around and thought, *What if I decline? Will she take Ahmed and me as ransom to assure a quicker surrender of the Alhambra?*

He looked around him and saw himself surrounded by soldiers. He had no choice but to accept.

"If you insist, kind Majesty, my son Ahmed and I will join you for a short merienda."

"I do insist," said the unrelenting queen of Spain sweetly.

Is she sincere? wondered the sultan. *What is in the back of her mind?*

~⌒~

Nonetheless, the king of Granada and his son came off the magnificent white Arabian horse with the white-as-snow tail that attracted the attention of all those present.

"The sultan's horse looks magical," said Lita Ledesma of Cordoba Carillo.

"What your horse's name?" pesky Maria asked in a very low voice, approaching it carefully.

"*Atika*," Ahmed answered. "It means 'pure.'"

"I'm very sorry the apple hit you, Atika," contrite Maria continued talking to the horse. "Believe me when I say I didn't see you there. But I want to make it up to you. I have another apple that I will share with you."

"Maria, leave the horse alone," said Lope Rodriguez de Santa Maria impatient to go back to their games.

"It won't take that long to feed him an apple," she said, petting the snow-white horse gently. "Atika, are you hungry?" she continued.

"Come on, Maria, let's go," Sancha Perez de Padilla said, gently pulling Maria away from the horse.

"Let her be," Lenor Lopez de Cacabelos said authoritatively. "The rest of us want to pet it."

"Here, take a bite," Maria told the horse as she offered it the tasty yellow apple, ignoring her annoying friends.

Most of the children were captivated and wanted to touch this breathtaking all-white horse.

༄

The queen watched and indulged the children for a few minutes before saying, "Children, I would like you to stay here while I take the sultan with me. Joanna, will you keep an eye on your sisters?"

Maria saw the quiet and strange dark-looking boy standing by David. She turned to David and asked, "David, what's your friend's name?"

"Ahmed," David replied, smiling.

"Hello," said Ahmed. He was a bit uneasy being the center of attention and clung tightly to the horse's reins with one hand while he petted it with the other, making sure the horse felt safe.

"Your horse is beautiful. Do you ride it often?" asked playful Maria.

"Yes, I love riding horses," Ahmed said proudly. "How about you? Do you ride a lot?"

"Yes," Maria answered. "I love it."

"Come to the Alhambra, and we will ride together," Ahmed said innocently.

Queen Isabella heard the last comment. "Be patient, Maria," the queen said. "When we are in the Alhambra we will all go riding."

The sultan knew what the queen meant. He felt very uncomfortable and became angry at the realization that soon it would be theirs. He clenched his fists and remained quiet.

"Oh, you will have such a great time. The Alhambra is heaven on earth with all its different rooms and gadgets, and it is as much fun to explore the underground tunnels. There is even a—" David had not completely understood the gravity of the situation.

Ahmed kicked David hard on the shin. He did not want David to say anything about the treasures until he had talked to his father about them.

"Ouch!" said David, touching his ankle.

"David and I played hide and seek in the underground tunnels. It was scary but fun," added Ahmed who gave a David a warning look.

"What did you mean to say, David?" asked Joanna, who never lost a beat.

"Oh! I meant to say that there are fun rooms with all kinds of bugs."

"Yuck! I don't like bugs," the youngest Princess Catarina said.

"Well, Catarina, you don't have to go," Maria said. "But I myself want to see the bugs."

∽

Queen Isabella changed her mind and decided to have the children follow her into the temporary royal residence. "Children, on second thought, it is better that we should all go in together."

The disappointed children wanted to protest. They wanted to stay outside and have fun. But in complete obedience to their queen, they remained quiet as they knew they had to do what the queen ordered them to do.

Joanna understood how the children felt, so she said with a smile, "Are you not thirsty? Come, let us go in."

Joanna picked up little Catarina and followed her mother who was talking with the king of Granada.

"Sultan, let my footmen take care of your horse while we all go and have some refreshments."

"I appreciate your offer, but I think it might be better for Ahmed to stay with the horse."

"Nonsense," the controlling queen of Spain exclaimed. "Let the child come and have some food too. I promise I won't keep you long."

Once again, the king of Granada couldn't object and had to go along.

"Come, child," the king of Granada told Ahmed.

Ahmed looked hesitantly at his father, not understanding his agreeing to join the queen of Spain for a snack.

"From one kingdom to the other, we must gracefully accept the invitation from the queen of Spain," the polite and proud king of Granada replied.

29

A Lizard Shakes
Catarina's World

～

They soon entered a small new building and, contrary to the spaciousness of the Alhambra, where the open-aired rooms led to other rooms through small oval doors. The rooms here, even though large, were dark and somber.

There, all the exotic red sofas were low to the ground; here, all the individual brown wooden chairs were austere and elegant but certainly not inviting to a friendly discussion.

A lady-in-waiting hurried to the queen and curtseyed. "Your Majesty, I am at your service."

Queen Isabella smiled and said, "Have you any news from my husband, King Ferdinand?"

"Yes, Your majesty," the lady-in waiting said. "The king should arrive shortly."

"Very well. Would you tell him we have guests, the sultan and his son?" the queen of Spain said. "We will be having some tapas in the throne room."

"Your Majesty, in the throne room?" the lady-in-waiting asked politely, unsure she had heard correctly.

"Yes," answered the queen. "It is a friendly discussion, yet an important one."

"As you please," answered the lady-in-waiting. She called some servants and told them to bring the snacks into the throne room and set them on the conference table.

The queen and the sultan entered yet another room sumptuously decorated with rich, colorful green-and-gold tapestries hanging on the wall. There were no couches, but many heavily carved wooden chairs surrounded two simple thrones. The dark chairs were somber and certainly not conducive to a favorable discussion—quite a contrast to the rich, cheerful, silk-and-velvet low sofas of the Alhambra.

To the sultan's surprise, the queen did not sit on the throne, but, as if greeting a great friend and not the foe that she saw the Moorish king to be, invited him to sit next to her and Columbus at a long table.

The Moorish king gently pulled insecure Ahmed to his side and said, "Ahmed, please come and sit by me."

Ahmed dutifully obeyed and sat by his father. He looked at David with a desperate look. Even though David was getting a lot of attention from the beautiful Spanish princesses, he saw Ahmed's discomfort.

"David, won't you sit by me?" Ahmed begged in a barely audible, pleading voice.

David heard him. He knew Ahmed felt uncomfortable in this very different environment and wanted to make things easier for him.

❧

"Maria, let's go ask Ahmed about the underground tunnels," David asked the bubbly little princess. "They were so much fun to explore. He will tell you all about them."

David and Maria went to sit right next to Ahmed. Maria was always willing to play a game and was very curious about all the games they could play at the Alhambra.

"Ahmed, tell Maria more about the underground," said David.

Ahmed was very happy that David asked him to tell all about the underground tunnels.

"What made you go in the underground tunnels?" Maria asked, curious to know why someone would go under a building.

"I lost Kadar, my blue-green lizard," Ahmed answered. "We saw it go down into a grid in the floor and thought it would be beneath the Alhambra. So we followed it there."

"Did you find it?" Maria asked.

"No," replied Ahmed, who continued with a complete description of the underground with its noisy dungeons with odd animals, ghosts, and secret rooms. His father was too busy with the queen to hear what he was telling the audience that had gathered around him.

❧

By now, all the princesses and their friends were captivated by Ahmed's detailed account of the exploration of the Alhambra's underground rooms and wanted to know more.

"Oh! I want to go there and see," Maria said enthusiastically. "Can you imagine the fun we would have playing hide and seek, seeing bugs and bats, and listening to mysterious sounds? When can we come?"

"Maria, don't you go without permission," Joanna warned her younger sister. "I hope you listen this time."

"I don't want to go," Catarina whined. "I don't like bugs."

"No one will force you to," said Maria. "Exploring caves is for big kids, not babies."

"That's okay, I'd rather play with dolls than bugs," Catarina said, crossing her arms.

"Well, I think exploring caves could be fun," Maria said determined to do so at the first opportunity.

Once again, Queen Isabella had heard part of what Maria had just said. "Maria, exploring caves is not something I want you to do. They can be dangerous," the queen said. "I prohibit you to go into any caves, even if they are in the Alhambra. I also forbid you to even think about exploring caves at all. Do you understand, Maria?"

The caring, motherly queen of Spain had spoken.

"Yes, *Madre*," Maria answered, lowering her eyes embarrassed.

√

All the children had stopped talking and were looking at the tomboy Maria, who suddenly felt ill at ease having been reprimanded in front of everyone.

"You can always play dolls with me and pretend you are in a cave," said Catarina innocently.

Just as she spoke, a green lizard appeared on the wall.

"Oh! Look, Ahmed," said David. "A lizard."

All the preciously dressed young girls screamed in unison, "*EWWWWEEE!* Someone please remove this ferocious-looking animal."

"Lizards are not ferocious at all. They are totally harmless. They like people but get very shy around them," David said.

"Really?" Catarina said in disbelief. "It looks like a mean dragon."

"They don't bite. They love to eat insects. Ahmed has one as a pet," responded a calm David as he went to the wall where the lizard was.

"Ahmed, have you ever gotten bit?" Maria asked delighted by the appearance of this little green dragon.

"No, never," Ahmed answered proudly. "I have had lizards since I was a baby."

∻

"You are not going to touch the green lizard, are you, David?" asked little Catarina. "It could be dirty."

"The lizard is clean," David replied with conviction.

"I still don't think you should touch it," Joanna said, agreeing with Catarina.

"Ahmed, you are the expert with lizards," David said. "They are fast; why don't you help me catch it?"

"I want to help too," said Maria excitedly.

Ahmed was very happy to be asked to help.

Everyone was watching—even the motherly queen of Spain, who loved all children. Columbus, though, was getting a little restless and wanted the meeting with the committee now, but he remained quiet. Again, he was being on his best behavior as he was hoping the queen of Spain would finally agree to finance his sailing trip.

Ahmed approached the lizard very slowly and stopped. He looked at it and moved back and forth, mimicking the lizard's movement as it watched Ahmed, David, and Maria very closely.

"What are you doing, Ahmed?" asked the curious Maria. "You are acting weird swaying like that."

"I'm connecting with the lizard. I'm mimicking him. I want him to realize that I will not harm him," Ahmed said. "So you and David should do the same movement back and forth like he is doing and approach it slowly. A sudden movement will scare it away."

"You are weird," Maria said. "But, whatever..."

"Do you have to catch it?" asked a sad Catarina. "Poor lizard."

"We will catch it and release it outside where it will be happier," answered Ahmed.

"Glad to hear that," Catarina answered.

Ahmed, moving slowly backward and forward, came right next to the green lizard. He moved his hand backward and forward until it was right over the lizard, which was still waiting patiently for something.

Ahmed quickly grabbed the green lizard that just as quickly tried to escape. By trying to escape, it got stuck between two stones and lost its tail while wriggling.

Maria saw the tail fall and, without any qualms, immediately picked it up.

"Yuck," screamed little Catarina. "The lizard lost its tail."

Maria came over to Catarina and teased her with the tail, tickling her cheek with it.

"*Madre, Madre,* help me. Maria is being mean," Catarina whined loudly.

It was not the queen of Spain who came to Catarina's rescue but sweet Joanna.

"Maria, why don't you take the boys and the lizard outside," Joanna said, trying to calm things down. "Maybe they can bury the lizard's tail?"

"Good idea," the queen said. "Why don't you free the lizard outside."

Joanna picked up Catarina and held her tenderly. "It's okay, *mi amor*," Joanna said warmly.

Ahmed was on his way out when he saw Catarina's fearfulness. He thought he could show her how gentle the lizard was.

"Catarina, see I'm holding the little lizard and everything is well," Ahmed said. "Would you like to see it closer?"

Unsure, Catarina hid her face in Joanna's chest.

"Ahmed, I'd love to pet it," Joanna told Ahmed. She wanted to take this opportunity to teach Catarina that lizards are harmless.

Ahmed brought the green lizard to Joanna, who touched the lizard very lightly. Slowly Catarina turned her head and silently watched Joanna pet the lizard.

"Try it," Joanna told Catarina, holding her hand over the lizard.

"Try what?" boomed a loud, unfriendly voice.

30

King Ferdinand Is Unhappy to Find Muhammad XII with Queen Isabella

ᕃ

Just as the boys were getting ready to go outside, the king of Spain entered the throne room like a tornado, bringing with him a possible storm of bad things.

"*Padre*, I'm so happy to see you," said Catarina, who had overcome her distaste for the green reptile. "See, I'm petting Ahmed's lizard."

"Ahmed?" asked the king of Spain, ignoring Catarina's shout of joy. "Who is Ahmed?"

"Ahmed, *Padre*, is the son of the king of Granada," Joanna answered. "He saved David who saved—"

Maria didn't give Joanna a chance to finish her sentence. She didn't want her father to know of their escapade into town because he would certainly punish her severely for it.

"A green lizard," Maria added hurriedly.

"Hmmm," the king of Spain said. "Who is this savior, David?"

"He came with Columbus," the queen quickly replied.

"I didn't know Columbus brought someone with him," the grumpy king said. "Ahmed, David, a lot happened during my short excursion into the countryside."

The king of Spain gave Ahmed a cold, scrutinizing look and went to the table where the servants had just brought dozens of small plates of various food: green and black olives, spicy sausage and cheese tortillas, mini ribs, clams and mussels, artichoke rice cakes, *gilda*, hot potatoes, and walnut-apple salad.

He picked up an olive and a tortilla and said, "I am ready for a bite."

"I can see that," the queen said laughing. "You have built up an appetite on your excursion."

∽

That's when the king saw the Moorish king and Columbus standing by her. He threw a quick quizzical look to the queen, who turned her eyes to the Moorish child.

The queen of Spain became nervous when she saw her husband come into the room with a fracas. She knew he would question why the Moorish king and his child were in their abode.

She, in turn, wanted to protect the Moorish child from his virulent words.

"Come, Ahmed," the queen said under the cold eyes of the caught-off-guard king, who didn't expect his wife to be so nice to the Moor's child.

She knew her husband would not be pleased with her decision to befriend the Moorish sultan and his son, but she also knew he would come around and understand her position. "Come and share some Castilian snacks with us."

Ahmed did not want to appear impolite by saying no, but he was still holding the little lizard. The queen had forgotten about the lizard when her husband had entered the room. Ahmed looked at his father, who was ill at ease in the presence of the severe king of Spain.

"Ahmed, let me have the lizard; I will take it outside," said Maria, who was standing by David and Ahmed. "You and David go join my mother."

Ahmed gave the little lizard to an overjoyed Maria, who could not wait to hold it. But Maria didn't go outside to let go the lizard, she kept it and was showing it to all her friends.

"Come, come, Ahmed," said the queen gently, inviting him to approach the table.

Ahmed was intimidated by the king, so he stayed in place not moving despite the queen's invitation.

"What are you waiting for?" the king of Spain asked in a gentler way. "The queen desires you to join her, and so do I. Let's join her."

"Okay," Ahmed said shyly.

The sultan suddenly became suspicious of the king's change of tone from unfriendly to an overly warm manner toward his son. *What is the king of Spain thinking about?* thought the skeptical sultan.

"Son, let's take a seat, have a few tapas, and then take our leave," the king of Granada whispered to his son.

The king and queen of Spain looked at each other as if planning something.

"I have some meetings scheduled," the king of Granada said, being very protective and wanting to make sure the king of Spain knew. "Unfortunately, we must take our leave."

David went to stand by the Moorish sultan.

"King Ferdinand, Queen Isabella, thank you for your kind hospitality," the sultan said again for the king's benefit. "We brought David back safely. He was one of your guests who found himself, after rescuing your daughters, on the road to the Alhambra where I came upon him by accident."

"Rescuing our daughters?" Ferdinand asked with surprise, looking at his wife. "What does this mean?"

"I will explain later," the queen said. She didn't want to add any fuel to the already delicate situation. "Don't trouble yourself with this matter. David was very helpful."

"We appreciate your bringing back David," said the king of Spain. "But since you are here, maybe we should talk briefly about the conditions of the surrender," continued the king, breaking the queen's promise not to undertake any political talk.

Queen Isabella bent over to the king and whispered something in his ear.

"The queen just informed me that she has already discussed another time to meet with you on the subject. So I will abide by that," the very austere king said. "In the meantime, let's all eat merrily. As you do, Sultan, we too have a meeting scheduled with a special council and Columbus, a business entrepreneur who would like to find new sea trading routes. As a matter of fact, I have a group of people waiting in the next room for the queen and Columbus."

The Moorish sultan let go a sigh of relief. *No talk regarding the Alhambra. The Alhambra was his for a little longer.*

The adults enjoyed the Spanish delicacies at a friendly and leisurely pace.

However, contrary to protocol, the noisy, happy children ate in a hurry. They knew mischievous Maria was still holding the subdued lizard. The plans to release it had changed when her father, the king, had come into the room. Now that they had eaten, they were anxious to follow her outside and watch her release the tailless lizard and, most of all, return to their outside games.

ை

"The children all get along very well; even Ahmed seems at ease, don't you think, Ferdinand?" Queen Isabella asked her husband.

"Yes. I have observed that," King Ferdinand said with a note of dark urgency. "We will have to have the children get together again soon. Remind me to talk to you about an idea I have."

31

The Sultan Fears for His Son's Freedom

❧

"**S**ultan, would you be in agreement with Ahmed staying here with us until January 2nd?" the king of Spain asked impulsively without consulting the queen. "It would be a long play date."

The Moorish sultan's ears perked up, his heart beat faster, and he knew the inevitable was about to happen. If Ferdinand had his way, the Catholic monarchs would keep his son as security against him surrendering the Alhambra sooner than later.

For him, the surrender was not negotiable beyond the terms approved. The Catholic monarchs would have to wait until he was ready. But he would never agree to leave his son behind. They could keep him, the sultan, but not Ahmed.

The queen was surprised by her sudden husband's proposition, which, even though to their advantage, was unnecessary for now as there were still a few days left to the agreed terms of surrender.

"First, we have our scheduled meeting with Columbus," the queen said. "Why don't we talk about this play date after?"

"The sultan wants to leave now," the king said. "We need to address this now, don't you think?"

The sultan glanced at his son for a minute. He could not and would not trust the Catholic monarchs.

Would he have a few more days with his son? He closed his eyes and said a prayer. *We have to leave immediately and go back to the Alhambra,* thought the king of Granada.

"I know the sultan needs to go," said the queen, looking at the sultan's son and then Columbus. "But there are still a few more days left to the agreed date of surrender. Let the child return home for now. You and I can discuss this later after our meeting with Columbus."

Reluctantly, the king of Spain relented.

"And Columbus has been waiting very patiently to meet the council that will hear all the arguments about his needs that will allow him to sail and find a new trade route to Asia," the serious queen said authoritatively. "So there is absolutely no time to discuss harboring Ahmed now."

Columbus had sat very quietly ever since the queen had found the sultan with David. He had witnessed the whole interaction between the sultan and the Spanish monarchs and could not get involved in this political game. He knew the moment belonged to them and the Moorish sultan. He needed the queen to be on his side. He just sat there listening and waiting, not wanting to disrupt any of the ongoing dialogue.

His moment would come as the king of Spain said a committee was waiting in the next room. They were important for influencing the king and queen of Spain's decision in supporting his sailing trip.

32

The Most Important Men of Spain Are Waiting to Meet Columbus and the Queen and King of Spain

⤸

A servant came to the king and queen of Spain and announced that Marchioness de Moya, Duke Luis de Cerda, Alonso de Quintanilla, Mendoza, Gonzalez de Cordoue, Alessandro Geraldini, Martin Behaim, Abraham Senior, Isaac Abravanel, Doctor Jose Vizinho, and Abraham Zacuto had arrived. The servant knew the queen was very meticulous and always insisted on knowing the names of everyone attending her meetings.

"Thank you. Tell the committee we will meet now," the queen said. She wanted a change of mood. She had seen and talked to the sultan, and that subject was closed for now. They needed to go back to the matter at hand: Columbus's need of money to finance his sailing.

The servant stood there waiting patiently.

"Is there something else?" the queen asked.

"Abraham Zacuto would like to see Columbus right away," the servant said.

"Oh!" the queen said.

"He has brought with him a unique copper astrolabe he invented that he seems impatient to share with Columbus," the servant told the king and queen of Spain. "He has also brought several books."

"Tell Rabbi Zacuto that we will convene shortly," the queen said, not understanding this urgent need.

"What a great idea to have brought his latest invention!" Columbus said enthusiastically. "Your Majesty will enjoy seeing this new instrument that's invaluable to any sailor."

"You should check all the incredible instruments in the Alhambra," David interjected enthusiastically, not understanding the implications of his comment. "There are quite a few astrolabes, which, Columbus, you would love to see, I am sure."

The sultan smiled proudly but didn't extend an invitation to Columbus, and Columbus didn't ask to see them, even though he would have very much liked to visit the observatory. It would be a faux pas for him to bypass the queen of Spain.

⤳

Feeling an awkward moment, the servant decided to turn the attention back to the meeting that was going to take place between the scientists, the finance committee, Columbus, and the Catholic monarchs.

"Where would you like the team to peruse and discuss those books brought by Rabbi Zacuto?" the servant asked Queen Isabella.

"We must have them come in immediately and meet with us here," the queen said eagerly, happy to take the attention off the Moor. "We must hear everything the famous astronomer has to say about the probability of Columbus's success of finding a new sea trading route."

"I am as impatient as you are, my Queen, to hear about the possibility of the sailing," the king said in a more relaxed manner, forgetting the Moor.

The king and queen got up first, followed by Columbus. While the table was being cleared, the sultan looked for an occasion to leave as did the children, who wanted to go back outside.

"I'd love to see this new astrolabe," David told Columbus. "You should see the fascinating room in the Alhambra filled with all kinds of instruments used to tell the position of the stars. You would like it. Please, Columbus, can I stay here to look at this new astrolabe?"

"It is not for me to decide," Columbus replied.

"David, you certainly can stay, but so can everyone because everyone can learn from the scientists gathered here," said the queen, who enjoyed having the children close by whenever possible, unless it was a grave political meeting, in which case the children were excused.

Without consulting her unfriendly husband, the queen hurriedly said, "Sultan Muhammad, we enjoyed having you and your son. I understand you have a meeting, so you may be excused."

The sultan very politely said in a relieved but dignified voice, "Thank you, Your Majesty. With your permission, then, we will take our leave."

King Ferdinand wanted to keep the sultan and his son longer but couldn't differ with his wife in public. Looking irritated, the king nevertheless remained silent.

The sultan turned around ready to leave but couldn't.

The princesses were captivated by Ahmed's ways. They wouldn't leave him alone. So the Moorish sultan waited patiently close by for a few minutes before telling Ahmed it was time to go.

33

David Commits a Faux Pas

࿐

The servant brought a group of very serious and impressive people into the throne room, including philosophers, mathematicians, scientists, priests, and some wealthy Italians.

David was fascinated with the rabbi astronomer Abraham Zacuto, of whom he had heard so much. His uncle was a rabbi and had talked about what a brilliant Jewish Portuguese man he was. He said Zacuto had created a new metal astrolabe used by various explorers such as Vasco de Gama and Columbus. He also said that he had composed a famous almanac used by sailors and that he had written a history of the Jewish people.

"Don't you like having a moon crater named after you?" David asked Abraham Zacuto, so excited to meet the great Jewish astronomer and mathematician that he forgot for a minute he was in 1491.

A heavy silence fell in the room.

"What is the child talking about?" asked King Ferdinand.

The children as well as the adults became quiet and looked at David.

"I don't know, Your Majesty," answered the famed rabbi astronomer. "I want to hear what else the child has to say about it."

"David, we all want to hear what you mean that there is a crater on the moon named after Zacuto," repeated the king.

David now felt uncomfortable. *Crater* was an unknown word in 1491. How was he going to correct this innocent blunder?

"What is a crater?" someone asked, breaking the heavy silence.

Where David came from, five hundred years had passed since Abraham Zacuto had met the Catholic monarchs, and lots of discoveries had been made.

He was back in a time where the word *crater* did not exist until 1605. So the crater was named after Zacuto long after 1491.

"A crater is a dip, a large hole in the ground," said David, who had no choice but to define the word. He avoided saying, "a hole on the moon."

David took an olive and threw it in a bowl of whipped cream. "See the dip?"

"Yes," replied Maria as ebullient as always.

"That's a crater," David said.

King Ferdinand looked skeptically at David while asking Abraham Zacuto, "Is that true, astronomer Zacuto?"

Zacuto did not want problems for David.

"Yes, Your Majesty, a few scientists have used the word *crater*, but not with my name unless they were joking," he said smiling. "But, Your Majesty, let me show you my new astrolabe, which, along with the charts, shows ways to compute the position of the sun, moon, and planets relative to fixed stars and will make a success the sailing trips Columbus wants to undertake."

❧

Abraham Zacuto presented his new copper astrolabe to the king of Spain, who did not really know what to do with it. He showed it to his wife, the queen, who favored Columbus's desire to put Spain on the map with new discovered worlds. She did understand the astrolabe was instrumental to the success of his sailing.

She, however, did not have time to make a comment on the new, important instrument that would make it easier for sailors to find their way around the ocean, as she was interrupted by her son Juan, who had just come into the room accompanied by his teacher Luis de Santagel and the much-admired master chess player Luis Ramirez de Lucena.

"Father, don't you hope Columbus brings back all kinds of treasures? I see you were looking at an astrolabe. Is that for Columbus? Is Spain going to give Columbus the astrolabe?" asked the well-educated, thirteen-year-old future king of Spain. "He will need that to navigate the seas. The fifteen stars on the wind rose of the astrolabe will help tell where he is, and he will also be able to calculate the height of the sun, so he can navigate successfully."

While the queen's son was talking science, David wanted to tell of all the treasures in the underground tunnels of the Alhambra that could pay for Columbus's expensive undertaking, but the treasures were his and Ahmed's secret.

David understood that Ahmed first needed to make his father, the Moorish king, aware of what was going on under the Alhambra. He gave a quick glance at David, who with his eyes was begging him to be silent. But David knew better than to talk about the wealth located under the Alhambra.

"I know about men; my son knows about the stars," said the Spanish king, losing his grumpy mood and laughing.

"Thank you, Father, I'm a good listener," the serious king of Spain's son said laughing. "I have been present most times when astronomer Abraham Zacuto and Christopher Columbus discussed sailing to a new world. I myself am so captivated with Christopher Columbus that I'm ready to sail the world with him if, of course, Spain finances his voyage."

"I want to go too," Maria said. "Can I?"

"Juan, being aware of what is going on in the world, wanting to make changes, and being in the forefront of new things are important to rule a kingdom," Queen Isabella said smiling. "However, unfortunately, sailing is not part of your education. You will be a great king by observing us here in Spain."

Then the queen looked at Maria affectionately and said, "I am sorry, Maria. I know you like adventures. But you will be queen one day, and you cannot learn to be a queen by traveling the seas. You need to learn those skills at home from me."

"If you say so," Maria said, disappointed. "It would be so much fun being on a ship. I am not sure I want to be queen."

"We would miss you too much," Joanna said. "Much better if we all stay together and learn to be queen side by side."

"Maybe..." Maria replied uncertainly.

လာ

David could not resist adding his own words of wisdom: "Even though I will never be king, I'm always fascinated learning about how the world works. Juan, have you seen the observatory in the Alhambra? Sorry, I meant to ask if you have seen the interesting room in the Alhambra with all kinds of fascinating instruments used to measure the position of the stars."

"No, I have never been at the Alhambra," said the young future king of Spain grandly. "But I will soon," he added provocatively.

The sultan and Ahmed, who had not yet left the throne room, looked up, honored that David should speak so highly of the magnificent Moorish palace but distraught by Juan's defiant words.

"No one in our family has been there yet," said King Ferdinand harshly.

౼

Queen Isabella appreciated the distraction from the eventual surrender of Granada, but she felt the mood was changing and wanted the meeting to get under way.

The team of people assembled in front of her to determine the fate of Columbus's voyage was the best. She herself was convinced that the voyage would be good for Spain, but her husband, King Ferdinand, was more interested in fighting battles on land and protecting their lands than in conquering countries in other parts of the world. How would she be able to bring him to her side? Maybe the team that had been convoked would finally persuade the skeptical king.

The famous astronomer and his assistant had brought all the tools necessary to show the queen and king of Spain and their court how possible it was to make a sea journey successfully.

The philosophers and Cardinal Mendoza were there to debate if the trip would be a rewarding and favorable endeavor.

The Italian financiers wanted to hear how the seafaring adventure was a possible money-making proposition and also what Columbus would bring back to make this partnership with the Spanish monarchs profitable. So far, they had been open-minded about Columbus's ideas and were willing to fund part of the trip. But they wanted to hear more.

Ferdinand II's Jewish finance minister Luis de Santagel was there. He was convinced that Columbus's plans would be lucrative for the monarch's treasury. His opinion was crucial to this meeting.

ᴄᴏ

All eyes were on Columbus and the Catholic monarchs.

Except David's.

David's eyes were on certain men gathered in the throne room. The most important men in the room were all showing a round, yellow badge on their chest. Some of them were wearing a small yellow cap and a yellow belt.

Part of their outfit bothered him. *Why were people wearing that symbol in 1491?*

David knew they were Jewish by the yellow badge they wore that meant to identify their religion and separate them from the Catholics. Still, he wanted to ask why these men were wearing those yellow badges in Queen Isabella's court, but Columbus was talking.

Columbus said confidently, "I have here the astrolabe and the charts to guide me to a new world filled with gold and silver treasures that will make Spain one of the richest countries in the world. I even brought an interpreter Luis de Torres, who is willing to sail with me and translate if need be."

Everyone was smiling and dreaming of coffers filled with unimaginable riches.

"Unfortunately, there is an important official missing today," Queen Isabella said. "The monk named Juan Perez from La Rabida Monastery has been delayed. We, the king and I, will listen and hear all arguments, but we will have to hold off our final decision until he gets here."

"But, my Queen, my finance minister Luis de Santagel is here. Isn't that good enough?" said the impatient king of Spain, who very often didn't agree with the queen and didn't care whether the monk was there.

Ignoring her difficult and unwilling husband, King Ferdinand, the still-beautiful Queen Isabella, dressed in a magnificent emerald-green silk dress heavily embroidered with diamonds, rubies, yellow topaz, and quartz with a stunning green emerald and tourmaline diamond necklace adorning her elegant neck, turned her beautiful blue eyes to Columbus, who had been pursuing her relentlessly for more than six years.

"Dear Columbus, I know you want an answer now," said the uncomfortable, but very pretty Queen Isabella. "I can't give you an answer now. But I promise it will be soon." Columbus looked at her. "I have been waiting a long time, Your Majesty," he said with a ray of hope. "What is a few more days?"

"But please understand our dilemma. We have been busy fighting the Moors and making Spain a united Catholic country," the queen said. "This ocean voyage will require you to employ lots of people and lots of ships to navigate the seas safely. All this requires lots of money that we are short of at the moment. Spain needs money to rebuild and protect itself from future threats," continued the queen of Spain softly. "And we need to make sure that the trip is doable."

"I understand," Columbus said, relieved the queen had not told him no.

"I'm so much in favor of your adventure that I am willing to sell all my jewelry to fund your mission, which not only would have you find gold, but add many souls to God's realm. But I'm not sure the time to give you our final decision is today," the smiling, very clever queen added warmly.

"There are many ways to finance Columbus's sea travels," said the wise, older Spanish banker Abraham Senior.

"I agree with you, Abraham. It won't be necessary, Your Majesty, to sell your jewelry," Luis de Santagel said. "The jewelry is part of Spain's history. Why should you part with history? I'm willing to use some of my own funds to finance the voyage."

Columbus was getting very excited. It seemed all he needed was for the monk Juan Perez to talk to the queen and to the king.

                                    ✑

"How about playing your favorite game while we wait?" asked King Ferdinand, looking at all assembled there. "A game of chess."

All eyes were on the king and queen.

"Well, my Queen, would you like to play me a game?" the king asked. "It is always a challenge to play with you."

Before the queen could reply, their son Prince John said, "Father, why not challenge my mentor Luis Ramirez de Lucena, the best chess player in Spain?"

King Ferdinand examined the young Luis Ramirez and asked, "You are young—what makes you think you can play the king of Spain?"

"Well, Your Majesty, I have been playing for a long time, and even though I am young, I just started writing a book about the rules of playing chess because no one has written one yet," Luis Ramirez answered. "So, it would be a great honor for me to play with someone as good as Your Majesty and try some of the hundred and fifty moves I'm familiar with."

"I am an avid player, but I don't know half as many rules," the king said not sure he should play a younger man of no meaningful standing. "I'm dying to see what other rules can benefit my playing and make me win every time."

"And so is my wife. Why don't you challenge her to a game?" the king added, not wanting to be challenged by a much-younger man of no meaningful standing just in case he lost.

"That will be an honor," Luis de Ramirez said. "I have been inspired by Her Majesty the Queen's military exploits, and with those exploits I came up with some of the moves that makes chess exciting."

"I am flattered my military skills have inspired you," the queen said, always up for a challenge. "It will be a pleasure to play your new ideas."

"Chess is so much fun," David told Columbus. "I want to learn more moves. I know how to play, you know."

Everyone gathered around the queen and Luis Ramirez de Lucena, the chess whiz, and watched in awe at the duel going on.

The children were in attendance but they were not interested in the game of chess. They were still enraptured with the little green lizard and the exotic-looking prince Ahmed, who was ready to take his leave.

But David was interested in the game of chess.

ᥱᷤ

However, David was still troubled by all the men in attendance wearing a yellow badge—half of the men in the room were. Were these men forced to wear a badge?

And even though the queen was playing a serious game of chess, she was talking to Luis de Torres about his interest in following Columbus on his travels.

So, David took the opportunity to ask Columbus, who was, unfortunately, standing next to the king, who was watching the queen's every move. "I am very, very confused. The king and queen seem to really like the Jews. They are everywhere in this room, and they know they are Jewish. Why then are the Jewish men wearing yellow badges in their presence?"

Columbus did not answer, afraid the queen and king would hear.

David had a heavy heart. "I'm Jewish, and I know bad things have happened to people that wear yellow badges. I don't understand why the queen and king of Spain trust Jewish people and surround themselves with them, and yet they are going to force them to live a different life and leave Spain if they don't obey them," David said innocently. "Why, Columbus? Please tell me. It is so unfair to them."

The queen had heard, and so did the king.

"Because as a Catholic queen who has fought many years to have a united country dedicated to Jesus, why would we allow the Jews to continue to live in Spain as non-Catholics?" the queen said in a firm voice.

"David, how do you know we will expel the Jews who refuse to convert?" asked a puzzled King Ferdinand.

☙

"Yuck," screamed little Catarina.

"Maria, take the lizard off me. Get it off; get it off me," continued yelling Catarina.

The lizard didn't stay on Catarina long. It jumped off and disappeared.

Pandemonium ensued.

The children were shouting excitedly, looking for the lizard.

The queen stopped playing chess, which was a good thing since she was losing to Luis Ramirez.

The pensive queen was quietly observing David.

Columbus was very uncomfortable and didn't dare look at the queen. He had brought David along, so he was responsible for his actions. He was not happy with David and looked at him grimly, wondering what his chances were now for the queen and king of Spain to award him the money necessary for his trip. How could David question the actions of such great monarchs?

☙

The dutiful servants ran to comfort poor little scared Catarina.

"How can you be scared of this tiny tailless lizard?" Maria asked laughing. "All it wants is love. It does not want to harm you at all. And you touched it before, and you were fine."

"I just didn't like it on me," Catarina said.

"Look—it's on David's shoe," Joanna said.

All the children rushed to David, who still felt confused and sad about the Jewish men wearing yellow badges.

34

Columbus Is Mad at David

❧

But David was very, very smart and quickly realized that Columbus was distressed.

He knew how lucky he had been to spend time with Columbus because he got to meet Leonardo da Vinci, Michelangelo, King Henry VII, Anne of Brittany, Queen Isabella, and the Moor. He had had a lot of fun traveling with him, and now he had caused trouble for him by opening his big mouth and impulsively asking a question that he didn't know he shouldn't have. He saw Columbus's angry look and wanted to make amends. *Was the queen upset with Columbus?*

But what could he do to make the queen of Spain smile and not be mad at Columbus?

Quietly and very slowly, he bent down so as to not scare the little lizard that was very comfy resting there.

He picked up the little green lizard, holding it as if it was a most precious jewel. "Would you accept this very valuable but humble gift, Your

Majesty?" David asked ceremoniously, offering her the lizard.

The queen, looking at David's generous gift, couldn't hold her laugh.

Before the laughing queen could open her mouth to accept the gift, Maria jumped in front of the queen and said enchantingly, "Oh! Mother, let me accept this most esteemed present. I will take such good care of it."

The whole court laughed, even the crabby king.

"I forgive your impulsive behavior, Maria, as I know you are most trustworthy to take care of this most priceless gift," Queen Isabella said laughing. "Now run along with it and give it a suitable abode."

David smiled at Maria, who left happily, holding carefully her regained treasure.

David had one more thing up his sleeve.

"Your Majesty, I have something here that was given to me by a French monk at the Court of Anne of Brittany," David said to the intrigued queen. "It is a most beautiful rosary, which, as you now know, I, being Jewish, will not be able to use. But in your hands, this rosary could bring about miracles, I'm sure."

Under the watchful eyes of the Spanish queen and her court, David dug in his pocket and withdrew the beautiful hand-carved rosary to hand to the radiant queen, who was happy to receive such a magnificent and blessed gift. As he did so, the magic coin fell out.

"How beautiful this rosary is," the surprised queen said appreciatively. "I love the rosary, and I will pray with it that God always helps me make the right decision."

"I was told to use the rosary because it had special power in time of need," David said. "Hopefully it will help you."

૯౨

The queen had seen the coin fall and was curious about it.

"But, what is this gold coin that fell out of your pocket?"

David was suddenly afraid to show the magic gold coin. The coin was his only way back home.

How would he explain having the coin in his possession?

What would happen if the queen wanted to keep it?

How would he get back home?

Hoping to disappear, he slowly bent down to pick up the magic coin while silently wishing, but nothing happened.

When he got up, he was still in the presence of the queen, who was looking at him curiously.

She was studying this strange blond, blue-eyed, and curious little boy, who had shaken her inner soul regarding the matter of the expulsion of the Jews, and who was holding a coin that had not yet been printed.

Who is this little boy that knows what nobody else knows, she thought.

"How did you come to be in possession of a gold coin with my picture on it? A coin that I have not yet seen because it does not yet exist?" asked the puzzled queen, who had been able to clearly see the coin.

"Ferdinand, come and see this gold coin with our effigies, a picture of both you and I," the agitated queen said. "We have been talking of striking a gold coin with both our effigies just like this one."

"You mean the 'Excelentes' coin?" the king asked.

"Yes," the baffled queen answered.

"I don't think it's a gold coin," David said, surprised to hear the queen say it was. "It's just a metal coin that I found in the dirt."

Columbus, fearing that another faux pas would definitely stop the religious queen from approving the sailing expedition, said, "Your Majesty, I have rescued David from possible abandonment. I have been caring for him until I return to Genoa."

Columbus did not want to tell the queen that David was a stowaway. What kind of a person would he appear to be?

"I'm still learning about his background. I don't know about his coin," Columbus said, defending David. "As my little assistant, he has, however, been a truly wonderful presence in my life. Diego, my beloved son, wasn't able to make the trip, so having David at my side filled a huge void. He has been like my second son."

As the king approached the queen and David, so did Columbus, who tripped on the king's foot. Columbus almost fell on David, who was just about to give the magic copper coin to the queen.

The coin fell down one more time. David bent down one more time to recover the magic coin. He picked it up slowly, closing his eyes, and wishing it had all been a dream.

"I'm happy to tell you, Your Majesty, that I must return David to the port where I found him just to..."

35

Was It a Dream?

Or Was It Not?

෨

David did not hear the end of Columbus's sentence.

"And this, children, is the first part of the story of the great explorer Christopher Columbus, who wanted to find a new route to Asia but instead discovered a new world called the Americas."

David, fully awake, was sitting at his school desk smiling and still holding the magic coin.

Where should I go next? thought David.

෨

The End or is it?

WHERE DO YOU THINK DAVID WILL GO NEXT?

$\sim$

Send your answers to paulinedesaintjustg@aol.com

Books in the same series:

Leonardo da Vinci, Columbus, and Little David

Michelangelo, Columbus and Little David

Henry VII, Prince Arthur, Columbus, and Little David

Anne of Brittany, Arnaud the Page, Columbus, and Little David

Made in the USA
Monee, IL
10 February 2022

91026989R00125